AL(EXANDRA) THE GREAT

AL(EXANDRA) THE GREAT

CONSTANCE C. GREENE

A YEARLING BOOK

Published by
Dell Publishing Co., Inc.
1 Dag Hammarskjold Plaza
New York, New York 10017

Yearling ® TM 913705, Dell Publishing Co., Inc.

ISBN: 0-440-40350-2

Reprinted by arrangement with The Viking Press
Printed in the United States of America

July 1983

10 9 8 7 6

CW

AL(EXANDRA) THE GREAT

CHAPTER 1

"Did you see that?" Al hissed, grabbing my arm so hard it hurt.

"Cut it out," I said. "That hurts."

"Now I've seen everything." Al let go of me. She shook her head in amazement.

We were on our way to the zoo in Central Park. School ended last week. Summer was upon us. You could almost see the heat rising from the pavement. The buses roared by, sending out great smelly clouds of exhaust. There were guys selling freshly squeezed orange juice on practically every corner. At a buck a throw, it *better* be freshly squeezed.

"What's your problem?" I said.

"That girl. Woman. Whatever. The one that just passed." We turned and looked behind us. Whoever she was she wasn't in sight.

"She must've dropped through a trapdoor," Al muttered. "Either that or someone dragged her into the bushes. She had the most incredible shape I've ever seen."

"What was the matter with her shape?"

"Well—" Al's eyebrows went up. "Well, it would depend on how you look at it. I didn't say anything was the matter with it. I simply said it was incredible."

"Don't be mysterious," I said. "It's too hot for mystery. Spit it out."

"She jiggled," Al told me.

"You mean she jogged?"

Al eyed me scornfully. "If I meant jogged, I would've said jogged. I mean she jiggled. Inside her shirt she jiggled. Like a bowl full of Jell-O."

"Probably she had big bosoms," I said. I've noticed that big bosoms jiggle more than small ones.

"How many could she have?" Al asked me. "It looked to me as if she had more than she could possibly need."

"She probably wasn't wearing a bra."

"With a shape like that she wasn't wearing a bra?" Al said disdainfully. "Good night nurse! With a shape like that she should not only be wearing a bra, but also an all-in-one, not to mention a chastity belt."

Not only did I not know what an all-in-one was, I also

had never heard of a chastity belt. They both sounded absolutely bizarre. But I wasn't going to ask Al. Not right away. Let her stew a little. It would do her good. She likes to use words she thinks I don't know the meaning of, and, unfortunately, she's usually right. She likes to throw them at me and then sit back and give me the bilious eye, waiting for me to say, "What's an all-in-one?" or "What's a chastity belt?" like some little wimp. Not this time.

I kept on walking.

"Did you hear me?" Al said, giving me one of her famous piercers. When Al shoots a piercer at me, I can almost feel it. She has the most pointed eyeballs of anyone I know. I decided to let her stew some more.

"Look!" I said. A person was slinking toward us. She was a symphony in blue. She had on blue satin pants, a blue sweat shirt, blue high-heeled shoes, and a tiny blue hat perched on the side of her head, looking as if it might take off at any minute. She also had blue hair. She looked like a chorus girl in a musical comedy. She also looked very pleased with herself. Nobody except us paid any attention to her.

We observed a respectful silence until she passed.

"That's what I like about New York," I said. "Where else could you see someone got up like that walking down the street and have hardly anyone turn to stare? I mean, where else? Certainly not in East Ely, Nevada."

"Who ever heard of East Ely, Nevada?" Al snapped. She was mad because she'd never heard of East Ely and also because I wouldn't ask her about the all-in-one and the chastity belt.

"It's a real place," I said. "My father knows someone from there. Look it up in the atlas if you don't believe me."

Al stomped along, muttering to herself. We stopped on the corner of Fifth Avenue and Sixtieth Street and watched a couple kissing each other like they were trying out for a part in a movie. Either that or they were kissing good-bye because one of them was going around the world on a tramp steamer and would be gone for about ten years. The girl had beautiful long red hair and wore jeans so tight she probably couldn't have sat down in them. The man had on a cowboy hat and a leather bomber jacket. In this heat. Insane. They were a very mod couple. Also very unselfconscious. If anyone ever kissed me like that out in the open and all, I would've died. It didn't bother them.

"Fools," Al said. "What do they know of love?" We crossed the street. On the other side Al stopped and said, "Don't you want to know what a chastity belt is? If you don't ask me before I count to ten," she said—"One, two," she counted—"I won't tell you. No matter how much you beg and plead, I won't tell you.

"Three," she said slowly.

"It's a belt to keep your chastity in," I said, taking a wild guess. "Sort of like a money belt," I added very firmly. I've noticed if people say something in a firm tone of voice, in a very convincing way, even if they haven't a clue as to what they're talking about, other people tend to believe them.

"I think they sell them at L. L. Bean's," I said, even more firmly.

"You think they sell chastity belts at L. L. Bean's?" Al said, pronouncing each word carefully.

"Yes. It seems to me I saw them advertised in the spring catalogue. I'm sure I did," I said, getting carried away.

Al laughed so hard she almost choked. Her face turned beet red, and I had to smack her on the back so she could get her breath.

"What's so funny?"

"It's—it's what you said. A chastity belt from Bean's. Oh-oh-oh." She clutched her stomach. "A chastity belt," she said at last when she recovered, "if you must know, is to keep people chaste."

"How can you keep people chased?" I said.

"C-H-A-S-T-E," Al spelled out. "That means pure. Virgin. You savvy?" She gave me a piercer.

"Boy," I said in my super-sarcastic voice, "they must sell a lot of those these days. From what I hear, at least one person in a thousand is a virgin."

"In the Middle Ages," Al explained slowly, as if I might not have all my marbles and she wanted to be sure I understood, "when the knights went off to war, they locked up their wives in these chastity belts to keep them pure until they returned. Which might be years from when they left."

She watched me to see what I thought about that.

"They locked them up!" I hollered. "Why didn't those wives tell them to buzz off? They had some nerve!"

Luckily, Al was in a patient mood. "They didn't say, 'Buzz off,' in the Middle Ages," she said. "They probably would've said, 'Begone,' or something like that. Maybe, 'Begone, sire.' That's the way they talked in the Middle Ages."

All of a sudden she's an expert on the Middle Ages.

"I never heard of such a thing," I said. "Why didn't they just whip off those old belts the minute the knights were out of sight?"

"Because the knights took the keys with them," Al told me. "And the belts—well, they were really more like a pair of drawers—were made of iron."

"Iron?"

"Yup. They locked them up and took away the key. How about that? That way they made sure there was no hanky-panky going on while they were out jousting."

"Then their wives should've decked them," I said indignantly. "I never heard anything so disgusting in my life."

"They did things differently in the good old days."

"That's the understatement of the week." We headed toward the monkey house to see the new baby monkey.

"Just tell me one thing," I said when we were halfway there.

Al stopped, crossed her arms on her chest, and inclined her head slowly, graciously, like a school principal giving a kid permission to ask one question.

"O.K. How did those virgins go to the bathroom? If they were locked into iron drawers to keep them chaste, would you kindly tell me how they went to the bathroom?"

Al stared intently into the distance, a sure sign she didn't have the answer. Joy filled my heart. I had her. I knew I did. History books *always* skip good stuff like that.

"Trust you to think of something gross like that," she said, glaring at me. "Trust you." She went charging down the path, and I followed, smiling.

CHAPTER 2

Outside the monkey house we filled up our lungs with enough air to last us. Once inside, we only breathe through our mouths, not our noses. The smell is something fierce.

The guard stood propped against the wall, watching us. Maybe he thought we were planning to rip off a couple of monkeys.

"Ask him," Al said, nudging me. She doesn't like to ask people things, directions, anything like that. She always makes me do the asking. I went up to the guard. He was new.

"Where's the baby monkey?" I said. "They told us last time we were here that the baby was coming in a couple of weeks." He just looked at me.

"There was this pregnant monkey," I said. "Has the baby been born yet?"

He folded his arms on his chest and kept looking at me. Just when I'd about given up and was preparing to look for myself, the guard said, "You got me. I'm part-time. I don't know nothing about no pregnant monkey. Come back when Larry's here. Larry knows."

"Where'd Larry go?"

"Atlantic City. Honeymoon. Him and the missus like to play the slot machines." He pushed his hat back on his head. His forehead stretched on and on, hairless and smooth. "They give you a good deal. You get your bus fare, your hotel room, a nice, classy-type hotel, breakfast thrown in. Plus," he said, "plus you get a free champagne cocktail. Courtesy of the management. All for thirty-six bucks a day, plus tax, double occupancy." He must've memorized the ad.

"Well," I said, "I guess if Larry and his wife are on their honeymoon, it must be double occupancy, right?" I gave him a smile, reluctantly. He didn't look like the kind of man who would know what to do with one.

"Yeah. Right. So come back in a coupla weeks. Larry should be back by then. I'm just filling in. Sure stinks in here, don't it?"

"It's not so bad if you hold your breath," I told him.

"Try holding your breath for five hours, the whole five hours I'm standing here," he said in an aggrieved voice.

Al was circling the room on her own.

"Hey!" she said. "Over here! He's here! Come see!" She was hanging on the bars of a cage, looking in at two gigantic monkeys who were busily picking fleas or lice off each other. They were really concentrating. Between them, almost squashed, was this little tiny face peering out at us.

"That's a face that only a mother could love," I said.

"I think he's adorable," Al said. "He looks sort of like Teddy." Teddy is my brother. He's nine.

"Boy, you better not let my mother hear you say that," I told her. I was sort of hurt. It would've been all right if *I'd* said the baby monkey looked like Teddy. But I didn't think Al should've said it.

"I'm sorry." Al can be very quick at catching bad vibes. "I meant it in a nice way. He's adorable. So's Teddy." She smiled at me. "And Teddy smells better."

"That's what you think," I said. We leaned on the bars and made dumb faces and talked baby talk to the little monkey. His parents kept picking stuff off each other. One thing about monkeys, they take care of each other. They have very strong family feelings.

On our way out I waved at the guard, who acted as if he'd never seen me before. "See you," I called. "We found him. In cage three. In case anyone wants to see the baby. Cage three."

He caught on I was talking to him and said, "Oh, yeah," but I doubt he was tracking. Probably he was thinking about Atlantic City and slot machines, not to mention double occupancy.

"Come home with me and watch me pack," Al said as we hit the street and breathed in the wonderful, polluted New York City air.

"Isn't it a little early to start packing?" I said. Al's going to visit her father and his new wife, Louise, and Louise's three sons: Nick, Chris, and Sam. That was one big plus for Al. She inherited three stepbrothers when her father married Louise. She really likes them. I only have Teddy. He's my blood brother. They say that blood is thicker than water. Whatever that means.

"You've got loads of time," I told her. "If you pack now, everything will be wrinkled when you get there." Al's leaving next week. She plans on staying for three weeks. They asked her for a month, but she doesn't want to leave her mother for that long. She and her mother might go on a cruise when she gets back from her father's farm. They're having a barn dance there for Al, with a fiddler and homemade ice cream. And the boy named Brian that Al likes will be there. It sounds exciting.

"Listen," Al said. "Don't think it's easy, packing for that long. Because it isn't. I'm only taking one bag. But I have to make sure I take the right clothes. I don't want to look out of place. I don't want it so's when I walk down the street, they look at me and say, 'Wow. Look at that creep. She must be from the big city.' I definitely don't want that to happen.''

Oh, boy. Al was going to get plenty heavy about her farm wardrobe. When Al gets heavy about something, she doesn't fool around.

"If you're on the farm all the time," I said in my soothing voice, "probably all you have to have is blue jeans and sneakers. And some T-shirts. Maybe a dress if you go to church or anything. And don't forget the white gloves," I said, kidding. Al got all steamed up when she went to her father's wedding to Louise. She was afraid her mother would make her take white gloves. Al's mother works in Better Dresses. She's very style-conscious.

Al frowned. "It's easy for you to kid around," she said. "But I definitely don't want to look like a city square. You have to be careful not to look out of place. Especially when you're from the city and you go to the country. You don't want the kids there to think you're a snob.''

"You couldn't be a snob even if you went to snob school," I told her. It's true. Al is very down-to-earth. She is practically the most down-to-earth person I know.

"You're a very down-to-earth person," I said. "Even if you went to Buckingham Palace to have tea with the Queen, you'd be down-to-earth."

"Maybe you're right," she agreed. I could tell she was pleased. People are always pleased to be called down-to-earth. I have to reassure Al a lot. She's a year older than me, but she still needs a lot of reassurance.

We headed across Fifty-seventh Street. There are a lot of art galleries there. Usually we stop and check out the paintings, chose the ones we wouldn't mind having if we could afford them. Which we couldn't. But today we didn't stop. I wouldn't have minded. But Al was in a hurry to get home and start packing.

"Come on," she said, charging along at a fast clip.

"O.K.," I said.

I'm not going anywhere. That I know of.

CHAPTER
3

Al and I have been friends for almost a year. Well, actually, about eight months. I feel as if I'd known her forever. When Al and her mother moved into our building, right down the hall from us, Mr. Richards was the assistant super. Then he died. Now we have one crummy assistant super after another. Mr. Richards was a retired bartender, a superior person, a prince among men. We miss him. He told us he thought we'd be stunners someday. We're still waiting. Al will be fourteen in August. I'll be thirteen in September. Al keeps waiting for something exciting to happen to her. I do too—to me, I mean. I think she's had enough excitement for a while. She's going to the farm, and she got a postcard from Brian, from Chicago, where he was on a trip with his 4-H club. Now it's my turn.

When we got off the elevator, I saw an envelope on our hall table. It was a letter from Polly. Polly stayed with us while her parents went to Africa. Now she's up on the Cape visiting her aunt and uncle. I tore open the letter.

"It's from Polly," I told Al. "She's having a blast. She goes sailing and swimming and clamming every day."

"That's not so much," Al said. "Write her back and tell her we went to the zoo and saw the baby monkey. That'll make her wish she was back here, pounding the pavements, smelling the good smells of New York in July."

Al did a couple of bumps and grinds and opened her front door at the same time. She's getting really good at her burlesque routine. We grabbed a handful of carrot sticks from the refrigerator and went into Al's bedroom. Her bed was piled so high with clothes it looked like a rummage sale was going on.

"What's this?" I pointed to a box of clothes sitting on the floor. On top was Al's brown vest. She only wears that vest when she's in the pits.

"Everything in that box is going outsville," she said. "It's nothing but stuff that freaks me out when I wear it. I'm sick of being drab, wearing drab clothes. From now on I only wear stuff that enhances my personality." She went over to the mirror and examined her gums to see if they were receding. She'd read about how receding gums are a big problem these days. Lots of people's teeth fall out due to receding gums, so Al keeps a close eye on hers.

"I'm heavyset," she announced after she checked her gums. "There are no two ways about it. I'm heavyset."

"What's that mean?" I asked.

"My features are not—how you say it in this country? —piquant. They do not sparkle. And another thing." She turned toward me, her face all puckered. I thought for a minute she was getting ready to cry.

"How come my hair doesn't move?"

I didn't say anything. I figured she really didn't expect me to.

"I use conditioner, the way they tell you to. I wash my hair so much it's a wonder I'm not bald. So what happens? *Nada.* Zilch. When I move my head, my hair just stands there. Doing nothing."

When I first knew Al, she wore pigtails. Then she went to her mother's beauty shop and they styled her hair.

"In no way," Al said, spacing her words carefully, "in absolutely no way does my hair resemble the hair of one of those chicks in those shampoo commercials. It just stands there."

She tossed her head from side to side. She was right. It *did* just stand there.

"Did I show you this?" Al dragged out a sweater from her bottom drawer and gave it to me. It was the exact color of violets. I touched it. It was very soft, very beautiful.

"I bet it cost plenty," I said.

"My mother gave it to me. As a going-away present." Al put the sweater back in the drawer.

"That was nice of her," I said. My mother almost never gives me presents, going-away presents. Maybe that's because I don't go anywhere.

"I wish she wouldn't give me so many presents," Al said. She sat on the edge of her bed and put her hands between her knees and looked at them. "Sometimes I think she gives me a lot of things to make up for the fact she's not here when I come home after school. I think my mother suffers a lot of guilt feelings about me."

"Why should she? She's a good mother. Lots of kids' mothers work. Practically everyone's mother works."

"Yours doesn't," Al said in what seemed to me to be a cold voice.

"So what?"

"Nothing. But she doesn't."

"Yeah. All she does all day is lie around eating bonbons and reading dirty French novels," I said in a sour tone. Boy. What got her started on my mother not working? What was I supposed to do—apologize to her because my mother didn't work? Holy Toledo. I didn't like where this was headed.

"Hey," I said. "What's with you? How come you're feeling sorry for yourself? You've got a lot of things going for you. Here you are packing for a trip that sounds great. A barn dance and everything. You heard from Brian. You heard from your father. What more do you want? How come you're on a feel-sorry-for-Al kick?"

When Al gets down like this, for no reason, it makes me mad. She broods too much.

"I am not." Al went into the bathroom. I felt like leaving. One minute we're having a great time, the next she's in the pits. I don't get in the pits nearly as often as Al does. I don't know why but I don't. Maybe it's because my mother doesn't work. Ha ha. While she was still in the bathroom, I took the brown vest from the box and put it on.

"O.K. if I take this?" I asked Al when she came out. "As long as you're giving it away anyway?"

She frowned. "What do you want that old thing for? It's a mess."

"I want to keep it as a reminder."

"A reminder of what?"

"Of when you were young and in the pits. When you're middle-aged and famous, I'll take it out and show it to my kids and say, 'Al wore this when she felt bad. Then she gave it to me and she never again felt bad. She never got depressed again. Because all the bad feelings went with the brown vest.' How's that?"

She thought about it. She wasn't sure if I was serious or not. Neither was I. But I saw her lips twitch. Just a little.

"Sure. Take it. That's not a bad idea. Next vest I buy is

going to be bright orange. You know. The same color the school crossing guards wear. If that doesn't cheer me up, nothing will."

"Not only will it cheer you up," I said. "it'll also keep you awake. That is some color."

"I do believe," Al said earnestly, "that colors cheer people up. It stands to reason." She went to her bureau and pulled the violet sweater out, put it around her shoulders and tied the sleeves around her neck.

"Is that preppy or is that preppy?" she said, turning this way and that, like a model, so I could see how preppy she was.

"You better not tie that sweater around your neck when you get to the farm," I said. "They don't dig that kind of stuff in the boonies."

"You just said a very interesting thing." Al sat down on her bed again. "I have to watch my step when I get there. They talk about different things in the country. They have different interests. Like, for instance, I better bone up on feed and crops and weather conditions. That's the kind of stuff the 4-H club members relate to. Cows and horses and pigs. When you come right down to it, I know practically nothing about cows and horses, much less pigs."

"If worse comes to worst," I said, "you can always give them a shot of monkey talk. They don't have monkeys up there, do they?"

"I heard something last night on the TV," Al said. "It might be good to throw in if the conversation lags. I wrote it down." She went over to her desk and picked up a tiny piece of paper. She's always writing tidbits of info on tiny pieces of paper.

"Did you know," Al began, looking over the tops of her glasses at me, "that a female panda is fertile only twelve hours a year?"

After a bit I said, "That ought to do it. That might stir things up in farm country. You got any more of those lying around?"

"No," she said. "But I've got a few days left before I go. Keep your ears open, will you? If you hear any interesting animal facts, write 'em down for me, will you? I'd appreciate it."

I said I would. I sat and watched her pack a little while longer. At the rate she was going, I thought it was a good thing she'd started early. No sooner did she put something in her suitcase than she put her chin in her hands, thought about it, then pulled out what she'd just put in and put something else in.

"Hey," I said finally, "I've got to go home and fix meat loaf. It's just me and my father. My mother took Teddy to the cousins in Connecticut for a visit. You want to take potluck with us?"

"I'd like to," Al said. "But I better not. I promised myself I'd stick around every night until I go. My mother and I talk about stuff. We're better friends now. Than we used to be, that is. As a matter of fact"—Al gave me her owl eye—"last night we had a candid conversation about sex."

"You did? What'd she say?"

"Nothing I didn't already know. But I didn't tell her that. She really never got off the ground, but I gave her A for effort. I'll take a rain check, all right?"

"Sure," I said, and went home to make my meat loaf.

CHAPTER 4

It isn't very often that just me and my father are alone together. My father and I, I should say. I like it when we are. We talk about things we don't talk about when it's the four of us: the whole family. For one thing, we don't have to stop all the time and explain things to Teddy. Teddy needs a lot of things explained to him. When I said that to my mother once, she said, "You did, too, when you were his age. How else do you expect to learn things if they're not explained?"

It was a hot, sticky night. We had air conditioning only in the bedrooms. I opened the living room window. Even when the city is very hot, the street noises go on.

As a matter of fact, there are more of them in the summer because everyone who can't afford to go to an air-conditioned restaurant or an air-conditioned movie is out on the street trying to get cool. I hoped my father would take me out to an air-conditioned movie. Or a restaurant. I doubted the restaurant, though. We almost never went out for dinner. It was too expensive. And as my father invariably said, "I like the groceries right here much better than in any restaurant." My father is a very smart man.

On second thought, I wasn't sure about meat loaf. The thought of turning on the oven made me sweat more than I already was sweating. Maybe we'd have hamburgers instead. Hamburgers are always good. There isn't too much you can do to ruin a hamburger.

I turned on the radio and danced around the kitchen. "Glide, glide," I said aloud. Mr. Richards. One point for me. Al and I have this routine. Every time one of us says something Mr. Richards used to say, we get one point. That's what Mr. Richards used to say when he was trying to teach us to polish the kitchen floor the way he did. "Glide, glide," I shouted above the noise of the music. If anyone had heard me they'd have thought I was losing it.

I like being alone, but I wouldn't like to be alone all the time. I wouldn't like to come home alone to an empty house every day, the way Al did. But once in a while being alone is a luxury. For one thing, if I didn't know that Teddy was safely up in Connecticut, I wouldn't be dancing around the kitchen. Because he'd catch me at it and start imitating me. I can't stand it when he imitates me.

I took out an ice cube and ran it over my forehead and my wrists, the way my mother did. It didn't cool me off much. I hoped, for my mother's sake, not for Teddy's, that it was cooler in Connecticut. My mother was visiting her sister Tess up there. Tess has two boys, one almost exactly Teddy's age. Tess just got a divorce. She and my mother are two years apart. My mother is older, but as far as I'm concerned, my mother looks about ten years younger than Tess.

My mother has a cow if anyone makes a long distance phone call except on Saturdays and Sundays, when the rates are down. Once in a great while—a real emergency —she forces herself to call during the day when the rates are at their highest. Before Tess and my uncle got their divorce, I caught my mother calling her sister in the middle of the day. Quite a few times. Well, that's when I knew something serious was going on.

"Why is Tess getting a divorce?" I asked my mother.

"Because he fell in love with another woman," my mother told me. I've thought about that a lot. And wondered if my father would ever fall in love with another woman. Once I asked my mother if she thought he would, and she said, "He wouldn't dare."

I guess my mother and father will hang in there. I hope so. I know a lot of kids whose parents are divorced. I'm practically the only kid in my class whose parents aren't divorced—or at least separated. That used to embarrass me a little. I felt as if I had to explain why my parents were still married to each other. That was when I was much younger, of course, when I didn't like being different. I've matured since then. But all these kids would come back to school on Monday or after vacations and tell these fantastic tales about where their father had taken them. I knew this one girl who said she and her father had flown to Bermuda. Just for the weekend. Well, she wasn't even tan.

"How come you're not tan?" I asked her. She said, "It rained." This girl has a reputation for not telling the truth. Still, she showed me the shells she'd picked up on the beach they'd walked on during a downpour.

Another kid I know said her father took her and his new girl friend—who was named Clorinda, of all things —to Lake Placid to ski. She said her father and Clorinda stayed on the novice slope while she skied the intermediate ones and that Clorinda twisted her ankle first crack out of the barrel and spent most of the day sitting in front of the fire, drinking hot toddies. And holding hands with my friend's father.

Boy. If I get to go to Barnes & Noble to buy a discounted book, it's a red-letter day. Big deal. I've decided it cuts down a lot on the excitement of your life-style when your parents stay married to each other.

I guess you can't have everything.

I heard my father's key in the lock.

"Hi, Dad," I said. He was carrying his jacket. He'd

opened his tie and undone the first button on his shirt. That showed it was really hot out. My father is quite a tidy man. His sleeves were also rolled up. He has very muscular forearms, which he got from piloting a gigantic plane when he was in the Air Force.

"How about a shooter of Coke?" I asked him. That's another of Mr. Richards' sayings.

"No, but I'll accept a shooter of beer if you have one handy," my father said. He really looked wilted.

"Coming right up." He went to take a shower. I got him his beer. When he came out he looked much better, much less wilted. My father is not exactly handsome. He's not very tall, and he's going bald. But if we passed on the street I think we would smile at each other even if we were strangers. He has very nice manners, and his eyes are a beautiful shade of gray-green. I asked my mother once what made her fall in love with him, and she said it was the way his hair grew on the back of his neck. And also the way he smelled. I think the best thing about him is that he can laugh at himself. He doesn't take himself very seriously. The worst thing about him is that he puts too much importance on getting good marks in school. When I bring home D's in my report card, he always says, "You can do better." How does he know? I'm doing the best I can.

When I first met Al, she said she had a very high IQ but that she didn't work to capacity. She used to freak me out talking like that. A lot of the time I didn't understand her. She also told me she was a nonconformist, as if that were something very special to be, something that set her apart. She was probably right. There aren't too many nonconformists running around these days. That I know.

I don't work to capacity either. I don't know anyone who does. Except maybe the infamous Martha Moseley. She's a girl in my class who is not to be believed. In addition to all her other charming idiosyncrasies, Martha has a habit of flashing her report card in people's faces so they can't miss the tidy rows of A's and B's she's racked up. You should hear her carry on when she gets a B-minus. It's enough to make a person retch.

My father and I sat in the bedroom with the air conditioner on high and watched the evening news. Watching the evening news with my father is not the most restful thing in the world on account of he doesn't happen to agree with anything the President says or does. He talks to the screen the entire time the President comes on the telly. Or the Secretary of State. He really has it in for the Secretary of State. This was going to be one of those nights.

"Oh, yeah," my father said in the special voice he reserves for talking to the President. "That's your story. Just go on the way you're going and you'll be out on your ear. Just continue robbing the poor and handing the money to the rich. Then try to get re-elected. Just try." My father chortled at the mental picture of the President trying to get re-elected. I went to the kitchen and started making the hamburger patties. I make a very neat patty,

29

with no uneven edges, if I do say so. I could hear my father talking a mile a minute, as if he had several guests.

As I took out a package of frozen broccoli from the freezer, I decided I would find out what my IQ was. By hook or by crook. I hope it doesn't turn out to be a disappointment.

CHAPTER 5

The next morning I zapped down the hall and rang Al's bell. I couldn't hear anyone moving around inside. I put my ear to the door. Nothing but silence. Maybe she'd overslept. Her mother usually left for work about a quarter to nine. Maybe Al was packing and unpacking her suitcase one more time.

I rang again. The door opened. Slowly, reluctantly. Al stood there, looking at me. She still had on her pajamas.

"My mother's just leaving," she said. She made a face at me. Her mouth was thin and sort of pinched looking, the way it gets when she's tense or nervous.

"I'll come back after she goes," I said.

"No, that's O.K. Come on in," Al said. Her mother was leaning toward the mirror, putting on her lipstick.

"Hello, dear," she said. She always calls me "dear." I used to think it was because she didn't know my name. But once when Al was away I visited her mother and we became friends. She calls me "dear" because she likes me. I know because Al told me. I like her too. It's easy to like someone when you know they like you. As a matter of fact, it's hard not to.

Al stood and watched her mother, her arms folded on her chest, a frown furrowing her forehead. I stayed near the door.

"You come straight home tonight," Al told her mother. "I'll get dinner and you can go to bed early." Al's mother did look tired. And thin. But she's always been thin. She says thin people look better in clothes than fat ones. When I first knew Al, she talked about wearing Chubbies, which are clothes for fat kids. She was always eating fattening things, as if she wanted to get fatter. Then Mr. Richards began feeding us carrot sticks and stuff like that, and Al lost a lot of weight. Right now she's sort of in between. I'm skinny.

Al's mother kissed her and then she kissed me. She kisses people more than my mother does. My mother is not a kissing person. She only kisses people if she's known them practically her entire life. Or if she really likes them. *Really* likes them, I mean. She's just not a kisser.

"You smell good," I told Al's mother. She always did,

due to the fact she put so much gunk in her bath water (she called it a "tub").

After she'd gone, Al said, "She doesn't feel so hot. I tried to get her to stay home from work today. But she wouldn't. She thinks if she stays home one lousy day, that store will collapse. But she has this cough that won't go away. I'm worried about her."

"I didn't hear her cough," I said.

"Stick around at night. She coughs practically all night." Al began to pace. "Last night," she said in a dark voice, "last night she went out with Mr. Wright and got home late. Very late."

Mr. Wright is Al's mother's new beau. She gave Ole Henry Lynch the mitten and now she's going out with Mr. Wright. When Al first told me about him, she said she thought he might be "Mr. Right." In the olden days, Al said, girls used to sit on the front porch knitting and waiting for Mr. Right to come along. That was back in the days when girls got married a lot. They got out of school and then they sat and waited for Mr. Right. Bizarre. What I want to know is how did they know he was Mr. Right. He could just as easily be Mr. Wrong. Or Mr. Rong.

When I had asked Al to come for potluck last night with me and my father, she'd said she was sticking around every night until she left for the farm. I guess maybe her mother didn't know Al was going to do that. Stick around, I mean. She must not have known.

"You want a croissant?" Al asked me. "Vi brought some home from this really classy pastry shop where everything is so expensive it makes your hair stand on end. But delicious." The stuff is so delicious it practically makes tears come to my eyes. Vi is Al's mother's name. Short for Virginia. Al only calls her mother by her first name behind her back. She says she doesn't think her mother is ready to be called Vi to her face. She's probably right.

We each had half a croissant and a cup of tea.

"She ought to know better at her age," Al said in a severe voice. "I told her she should know better. Especially when she's not feeling so hot."

Al suffers a lot from role reversal. I think having no father around or any kind of sibling, she sometimes feels as if she's her mother's mother and has to take care of her. I guess a lot of kids who live with just their mothers get into that habit. Sometimes, when Teddy is being more of a pain than usual, or when my mother and father have a fight and my mother has to lie down with one of her migraine headaches, I think it would be wonderful if it were just me and my mother. It would simplify life, I figure. This only happens to me once in a while, though.

Now I could see Al was worried about her mother. And from what she'd said, her mother had stood her up last night. I felt bad about that, but I didn't say anything. We took our dirty dishes out to the kitchen. There was a pot on top of the stove.

34

"What's that?" I said, bending down to sniff.

In a flash Al whipped the pot out from under my nose. She hurled it into the sink and filled it with water.

"Oh, that's just something I tried out," she said. "For last night's dinner. For laughs. It didn't turn out too well. As a matter of fact, it was a bomb. I could hardly get it out of the pan. I guess I had the heat too high. Either that or I didn't add enough liquid."

She bent over, scrubbing out the pot. Her hair hung down into the sink, almost touching the dirty water.

"Why don't you let it soak?" I said.

She kept on scrubbing.

"It didn't matter anyway," she said in a muffled voice. "It was only me. I had eggs."

CHAPTER 6

"I think what I'll do is," Al said. She paused for breath. We came out into the terrible street heat from the cool of the Donnell Library on Fifty-third Street. It was like fighting your way against a strong current as we beat our way uptown. Passersby looked harried and exhausted and as if they wished they were lolling on the sand, the ocean lapping at their toes, and they were eating an ice cream cone and telling their kids not to go out too far.

"I think what I'll do is," Al said again. And stopped.

"For Pete's sake," I said crossly, "don't do that. I can't stand the suspense."

"I'll shake hands," Al said in a rush. "With Brian. If

he comes to meet me with Louise and the boys and my father, that is. If he doesn't come to meet me—well, that's a different kettle of fish. That's a whole other ball game. I'll stick out my hand and say nonchalantly, 'Hey, Brian. Long time no see,' and shake his hand. What do you think?"

"Listen," I said. "A girl can't be too careful. You don't want him to think you're engaged or anything."

"Don't be wise!" Al snapped. "Either I shake his hand or I could just give him a little playful punch on his arm and say, 'How's tricks?' On the other hand, I don't want to be too casual. It's a tough decision."

I envied Al. I envied her her trip to the farm, and the fact that she had a boyfriend. Not a real boyfriend but a friend who was a boy, who sent her postcards. It meant she was grown-up. Always before we'd been even steven. Now she was moving on, moving away, doing grown-up things. Things that I had never done. I hadn't realized I envied her until that very minute. I wasn't sure I liked envying Al. But there it was.

"If that's the toughest decision you ever have to make," I said, trying to keep the sourness out of my voice, "you'll be all right. Aren't you excited? About going, I mean?"

Al began twisting a strand of hair around her finger, twisting it around and around so that it would be all snarled when she tried to comb it. That was a sign she was nervous. If she was nervous *now*, what would she be when she finally arrived? Boy, was I glad I wouldn't be

37

around for *that*. She'd be such a wreck she'd have to go to the bathroom every two seconds.

"It may never come to pass," Al said. "I have this feeling in my bones, you know?"

"No," I said. "I don't know."

"Well, it's too good to be true. The whole thing: the barn dance, Brian, the farm, the whole shmeer. I try not to get my hopes too high. To expect too much. Even if I do really get there. I tell myself it'll be a washout. That way, if something bad happens, I won't be too disappointed."

"Don't be such a killjoy," I said crossly. "Why can't you just relax and enjoy yourself, enjoy the anticipation? You're doing exactly what you did before your father's wedding. The exact same thing. Remember? You kept trying to decide if you should go or not. Back and forth, back and forth. If it hadn't been for me telling you you should go, you might not've. Then just think what you would've missed." I glared at her. "You would've missed the really big event in your life. You would've missed meeting your stepbrothers. You would've missed—"

"Hold it." Al held up her hand like a traffic cop. "Hold it. I get the idea. You're right. I agonize too much. I can't help it. I wish I didn't agonize."

"It will turn out to be beautiful," I said. "Perfect. The way the wedding turned out to be perfect. This will be the same. You'll see."

"Maybe." Al kept her head down as if she were

looking for money on the sidewalk. "Maybe," she said doubtfully.

We crossed Fifth Avenue and walked past this terribly chic Italian shop where the sales people have the reputation of being the rudest in the whole city. Which is saying a lot. One time Al and I went there and she started spieling off her phony Italian to the salesgirl. Al threw her arms wide and went on talking wildly. After a second the salesgirl showed us to the door and said something in real Italian that probably meant "Get lost!" We laughed for about five minutes about that. But we didn't ever try it again.

Now we walked slowly up Fifth Avenue, past the blind man and his German shepherd who are always there. We usually put some money into the man's cup. Today neither of us had a penny so we walked past him and his dog, staring straight ahead, the way people do when they pretend something or someone isn't there. Then we looked in Tiffany's windows and decided to go through the revolving doors to look at the jewelry in the cases. There are always some big, burly men wearing brown suits stationed by the doors in Tiffany's in case someone decides to make off with a diamond necklace or two. Those men stand there, trying to be inconspicuous. Any baby could tell they were security guards. What I can't figure is why they all wear brown suits. It's like a uniform. They might as well wear a little sign saying "Guard" on their lapels.

"You first," I said as we leaned against the cases. It was her turn. I was first last time. Al always takes a long time to decide what she wants. Not me. I make up my mind fast. We checked everything: rubies, sapphires, pearls. But especially the diamonds. They get me every time. I could feel the eyes of the men in the brown suits on us. There were bracelets and earrings, gold cigarette lighters, even a swizzle stick made of gold. I asked the man what that was for, and he said, "To break up the bubbles in champagne."

"Boy," I said, "that's for the guy who has everything, huh?" And he said, "We also have one with a diamond on the tip of the swizzle stick for those who want to go all-out." I told him I'd have to think about it. Tiffany's is the best place in the whole city to go shopping.

I went back to where Al was. "I like that one," she said at last, pointing to a mammoth ring so big it would've covered her knuckle. "What is the price of that one?" she asked the clerk.

When the salesgirl told her, Al recovered quickly. "Our fathers are in oil," she said in a snooty voice. "We're from Oklahoma." The clerk watched us, a little smile on her face.

"Try Saudi Arabia," I whispered.

"Would you believe Saudi Arabia?" Al said. Slowly the clerk shook her head.

"Oh, well. It's in rather bad taste anyway," Al said. "Too gaudy. Thanks anyway," and we twirled our way through the revolving door, back out onto Fifth Avenue, past the brown-suited men who pretended they didn't see us, the way we'd pretended we hadn't seen the blind man and his dog.

"The trouble with Tiffany's is they have no sense of humor," Al said. We walked for a couple of blocks, not talking. Then Al said, "I don't care if Brian makes a lot of money. Money isn't important. Happiness is."

"Who's talking about Brian?"

"It's just possible," Al said slowly, "that we might get married." I looked at her in astonishment. She was serious.

"We'd live on a farm. I'd help him. I'd like that—to go live on a farm. Everything smells good there, I bet. Also, you can live a lot cheaper in the country than in the city. You can grow all your own produce, you have your chickens for eggs, your cows for milk. You live off the land. I think that'd be neat, to live off the land."

Holy Toledo. Here she was, not even fourteen, and already she thinks she's found Mr. Right. Just like the olden days. I couldn't believe it. One minute we're checking the stuff at Tiffany's, having a blast. The next minute she's talking about marrying a kid she met once and living off the land. I was momentarily shocked into silence.

We stood on the corner of Fifty-ninth and Lexington, across from Bloomingdale's, waiting for the light to change. A hot little breeze chased the litter around on the sidewalk and wrapped bits of old newspaper around our ankles like warm bandages. Under our feet, a subway train thundered down the tracks, making the sidewalk tremble.

"The thing that gets me," Al said angrily, "is I know I shouldn't go off and leave my mother. Not at this time of the year. There I am, living it up in the cornfields, picking strawberries still warm from the sun, and there's my mother, slaving her buns off, making a living for both of us. I feel like a crumb, if you want to know. An absolute crumb, going off and leaving her."

"I thought you said she was going on a cruise with Mr. Wright," I said. "That's what you told me. They were going on a cruise and having separate cabins and everything."

Al shook her head. "That fell through. I think it was too expensive or something. Anyway, she's not going. If it wasn't so blasted hot right now, it wouldn't be so bad. But I can see myself sleeping under a blanket at night while it's so hot here she can hardly breathe."

"You have a good point," I said without thinking.

She turned as red as a sunset.

"Can I help it?" she said, her voice rising. "Can I help it if they ask me to visit in the middle of the summer? Can I help it if that's when I have a vacation and the boys have a vacation? Besides"—she fixed me with one of her super piercers—"who ever heard of a barn dance in the winter? I ask you that!" She stomped ahead of me, taking giant steps. I let her get way ahead of me. Maybe she'd let off some steam for the rest of the way home.

When we got off the elevator, we could hear the

telephone ringing inside Al's apartment. She unlocked her door and got to it before it stopped ringing. I waited outside.

"It was my mother," Al said, coming out into the hall. "She's working late tonight on account of they're taking inventory at the store. I told her she was crazy. You'd think she was a vice-president at least. They don't even pay her time and a half for overtime when she works late. And her voice sounded lousy, and when I asked her if she felt O.K. she said sure, fine, but she wasn't telling me the truth. I could tell she wasn't."

"Come to our house for dinner," I said. "It's just my father and me. My mother and Teddy'll be home day after tomorrow."

"That would be nice," Al said. "Thanks a lot. I'd like that. I'll come over after I take a shower, all right?"

I zapped into my apartment. It was a good thing we lived so close to each other. That way she wouldn't have to fix eggs for herself again tonight.

CHAPTER 7

"Dad, you look burned out," I said. My father had gotten home early.

He nodded wearily. "That's as good a description of how I feel as any I ever heard." He settled down with his paper. "I'll be glad when your mother gets home. And Teddy," he added as an afterthought. I said I'd be glad when my mother got home too. I pointedly left out Teddy's name. I don't think he noticed, though.

Our doorbell rang. Two, then one, then two. The telephone rang at the exact same minute.

"You are on the horns of a dilemma," my father said. "Which one shall you answer?"

"It's Al, Dad. I invited her for dinner. Let her in, will you? Hello," I said into the phone. It was Thelma. Thelma is Polly's best friend on the West Side. I'm Polly's best friend on the East Side. And never the twain shall meet.

"I'm having this party," Thelma said. "Actually, it's no big deal. I've got these two extra boys. They're sorta twerpy but they *are* boys. You want to come." I wasn't sure if she was asking me or telling me. "And bring Al."

"When is it?" I stalled, making faces at Al as she stood talking to my father.

"Right now. This minute. We're having spaghetti." I know lots of kids who won't go places for dinner unless they know what's for eats. Spaghetti's the safest. Nearly everybody likes spaghetti. And it's cheaper than pizza.

"Bring records," Thelma ordered. "Come over as soon as you can. Wear any old thing." And she hung up. I hadn't even said I'd go. That was Thelma for you. She assumed people were dying to go to her party.

Thelma has a maximum amount of self-confidence. Since she got a shape and had her ears pierced—a dynamite combination, some would have you believe— there's no holding her. She was bad enough before, but now—wow!

"Thelma wants us to go over to her house to a party," I told Al. "They're having spaghetti."

"Why's she want us?" Al asked suspiciously. She's always suspicious when it comes to Thelma. "She never asked us before. Boy, she must be hard up is all I can say.

How come now? Is she having an orgy?" Then Al blushed and put her hand over her mouth. She'd forgotten my father was there. My father has a way of making himself invisible when he goes behind his newspaper.

"She says she's got two extra boys. Twerps but boys. She says wear any old thing."

"I usually do," Al said.

I could feel my father listening to us. His paper was quivering. He thinks Al's funny. Amusing, not odd. She makes him laugh. I went over to his chair and peered at him over the edge of the paper. He was. Laughing, that is.

"You want me to call her back and say we can't come?" I said.

"Boy, if Thelma says they're twerps, you better believe they're twerps," Al said darkly.

"The summer is off to a flying start," my father said. "I don't know how you stand the pace."

"Do you mind, Dad? If we go? I took the stuff out of the freezer. All you have to do is cook a hamburger for yourself."

"Go ahead," my father said. "I'm happy right here."

We zapped into my room. And even though Teddy was in Connecticut, I shut my door. Automatic reflex. Teddy lurks a lot. He also pretends he's sleepwalking when I have a friend over to spend the night. That way he figures he's got an excuse for prowling through the hall and eavesdropping.

"Did you tell her we'd go?" Al said.

"She didn't give me a chance to say no. But let's. It might be fun."

Al picked at her cuticle. "Those West Side types can be very boring," she said, frowning. "They take themselves so seriously. Something about living on the West Side makes people take themselves very seriously."

"They're into culture," I said. "But Polly doesn't take herself seriously."

"Polly is a citizen of the world," Al said. It's true. Polly's father is in the diplomatic service. She has been to a lot of exotic places. Polly plans on being a chef when she grows up.

"It wouldn't matter where Polly lived," Al said. "Polly's as loose as a goose."

"I wish she was going to be at Thelma's," I said. "But let's go anyway. We don't have anything else to do."

So we went.

CHAPTER 8

Thelma threw open the door.

"Oohhhhh!" she squealed. "It's great to see you!"

We were off to a bad start. If there's one thing Al hates, it's girls who squeal. That and people with wiggly behinds. Those are Al's two big hates.

Thelma came at us. It looked as though she was planning on pressing cheeks. The way women do. If she pressed Al's cheek, she might be sorry. Al might flatten her. I wouldn't put it past her.

We sidestepped and landed up in the hall. I could see myself in the floor, it was so shiny. Also, Thelma's hall was loaded with mirrors. They probably called it a foyer.

I've noticed if the hall is super-fancy, people tend to call it a foyer. There were mirrors on all sides. You could see yourself coming and going. You could never get out of that joint with your slip showing, that's for sure. There was a tall vase filled with those stalky flowers I hate sitting on a table. Glads, those flowers were called, although I'm sure I don't know why. There's nothing glad about them.

"I hope we're not too early," I said. I sounded like my mother. When you catch yourself sounding like your own mother, beware. You have to watch stuff like that.

Al didn't say anything.

"Come on in the kitchen," Thelma said in a loud voice. "I'm making spaghetti. Polly taught me how." We followed. Al and I fought for last position as Thelma led the way. Al won. She always wins things like that. She hid behind me. She's taller and wider than I am so it's not easy. But she has a way of crouching down and making herself small when she wants to. Thelma had on designer jeans. The name of the designer bobbed on Thelma's rear end.

"I just wore any old thing," Al said in a voice as loud as Thelma's. "I'm packing to go to my father's farm next week. All my good stuff is already packed." Thelma didn't answer. She was too busy introducing us.

One thing I really hate is coming into a roomful of strangers. I really do hate it.

There was a girl named Daisy and three boys named Ned and Tommy and Art. They were all sort of lolling around on the counter tops, eating M & M's and talking with their mouths open, talking around the chocolate. They barely acknowledged our presence. Thelma stirred the spaghetti and Al stayed behind me, using me as a shield. Daisy and Thelma looked like twins. In addition to wearing matching designer jeans, they had pierced ears that were plugged with tiny gold earrings. They wore identical perky little bows to hold back their perky hair. They were all talking about going to law school, getting their master's degrees. And going to Harvard for their M.B.A.s. It was like being in a foreign country.

Daisy said she was planning on being the president of a large corporation, which is why it was essential she have an M.B.A. Tommy had his heart set on being a successful corporation lawyer.

"Like my father," Tommy said, cramming in the M & M's. "My father makes big bucks. That's what I'm out for, the big bucks."

"Who do you think makes more money," Ned asked suddenly, his eyes glittering, "the president of General Motors or the president of Chase Manhattan?" General Motors got two votes, Chase Manhattan three. Al and I didn't open our mouths. I was afraid to look at her. I ate so many M & M's I didn't know how I could handle spaghetti too. Sometimes nervousness makes you eat too much.

At long last Al cleared her throat. I thought, Oh-oh. "How old are you guys, anyway?" she said.

They were all thirteen. I happen to know for a fact

that Thelma's birthday is five days after mine. Which makes Thelma twelve, any way you slice it. I could've been rotten and brought that up, but I didn't.

"How come you're already planning on how much dough you're going to make?" Al said. "You're not even in high school yet."

They looked flabbergasted. They looked at each other.

Ned said in a cracked voice, "You wanna be a big fish in a little pond or a little fish in a big pond?"

"What's that got to do with the price of onions?" Al asked him.

That shut him up. He didn't know what to say, so he threw another handful of candy into his mouth.

"Supper's ready!" Thelma cried. We all sat down.

"Perry can't come," Thelma said, tossing the Parmesan cheese around as if it were confetti. "His mother said he might be coming down with chicken pox."

Al looked at me. I knew what she was thinking. Scratch one twerp.

Al twirled her spaghetti around her fork like a pro. "What about you?" She pointed her fork at the boy named Art. Food seemed to have made her bold. Art was the only one who hadn't said what he was going to do to make big bucks.

"What corporation are you going to be president of?" she asked.

"Oh, I've got a trust fund," Art explained. "I'm going to direct movies. I might also write the script and produce the flick, too." He had little pudgy cheeks and little pudgy hands, and he wore a shirt with an alligator on it. The alligator shirt is the tip-off. If you see a kid wearing a shirt with an alligator on it, you can be pretty sure of his personality.

"My IQ hangs in there around one forty, one forty-one," Art said nonchalantly. "Also, I test real good."

"What're you going to major in—English?" Al asked him, her face blank.

He looked surprised. "How'd you know?" he said.

"Your grammar. I figured you for an English major." She smiled at him so ferociously that he blinked.

"Where are your parents, Thelma?" I asked nervously. I wanted to change the subject. My mother would flip if she knew I was at a party where there were no chaperons. My mother has a chaperon fetish.

"They're in the study," Thelma said. "They're playing bridge. They don't like to be disturbed when they're playing bridge."

Al kept sneaking looks at her watch. I pretended I didn't notice.

After the ice cream we played records. Thelma and Daisy danced. With each other. Al and I sat there, busily avoiding each other's eyes. I was sorry I'd talked her into coming. If we'd ever looked straight at each other, it would've been disaster. Al excused herself and went to the bathroom. Art and Tommy and Ned sat in a tight little circle, discussing their careers. With their heads together, their hands making swooping gestures, all they needed, I thought, was three big black cigars to complete the picture.

Al came back, and then I went to the bathroom. I locked the door and sat there for a while, wondering how soon we could go home. My stomach felt peculiar. Someone tapped on the door and said, "You all right?" so I knew it was time for me to rejoin the group.

The music stopped, and Daisy and Thelma sat down. I could feel Al glaring at me. She wanted to go. So did I. But sometimes it's hard to make the first move. Then Tommy said his family was taking him to the Riviera in late July. Ned said he'd already been to the Riviera. He clued the group in on a couple of three-star restaurants that he thought worth going to. Daisy said the month to go to the Riviera was August.

"Not August!" Thelma said, shocked. "It's too crowded in August. My parents always go in October."

My head started to hurt. Where was the Riviera? I'd never heard of it. I thought maybe it was in New Jersey, but I wasn't sure.

"Did you know," Al said. Everyone looked at her. I could tell from her face she didn't know what she was going to say next. Either that or she'd forgotten.

Al got her second wind.

"Did you know that in some Mediterranean countries," she said in a rush, "men stick their handkerchiefs under their arms, in their armpits, to get them nice and smelly. They don't use too much deodorant there, you know." She smiled around at us all. "Then they dance around and wave the handkerchiefs at the girl they want to put the moves on." She stopped, exhausted, I think. I know I was. The rest of them looked at each other. They looked as if they didn't know whether to laugh or cry. I excused myself and practically ran to the powder room.

When I got back, no one was talking. Al jumped up as if she'd been shot out of her chair.

"My father will kill me," I said. "It's getting late." Thelma ran with us to the front door. "Thanks," we said, "it was a blast." Thelma swung the door back and forth, waiting for us to go.

"If you want a taxi," she said, "the doorman will get you one."

"*Ciao*," Al said. "That's Italian for 'good-bye,' " she said to Thelma, baring her teeth in a terrible smile. The door closed, the elevator arrived. We got in.

"Where's the Riviera?" I said.

Al shrugged so her shoulders almost touched her ears. "France, Italy. Mostly France."

"Oh," I said, "I thought it was in New Jersey."

Al just looked at me.

My father had given us money to take a taxi home. He didn't want us out on the street late at night. It was almost nine. It felt like midnight. Just as we got to the corner, a crosstown bus pulled up. We hopped on. Luckily, we had the exact change.

"You didn't have to do that," I said as we walked to the back of the bus. "The handkerchief bit, I mean."

"Listen," Al said in a fierce voice, "if I'd had a handkerchief handy, I would've stuffed it in the alligator kid's mouth. Do you realize"—she fixed me with her most steely glance—"do you realize that Brian could've taken on all three of those wimps and tossed them over his left shoulder? He's got these gigantic muscles, from pitching hay and all. And Brian wouldn't wear an alligator shirt if you paid him," she said proudly.

"If he did, they'd probably throw him out of the 4-H club," I said, joking. I laughed at my own joke. It was the only time all night that I'd laughed. Al didn't smile.

"Farming is very strenuous, you know," she went on. "Those nerds would be wiped out after a half hour of doing farm work. That kind of work Brian does every day." For the rest of the way home she talked about Brian and his muscles. I began to think he must be a combination of the Incredible Hulk and Superman.

As we rode up in the elevator in our building, I said, "I think Thelma is trying to find herself."

"Yeah?" Al said. She fumbled for her key, which she keeps on a chain around her neck. "Well, when she does, tell her to get lost for me, O.K.?" She turned the key in the lock and opened the door. "Have a weird day," she said, doing a couple of pretty good bumps and grinds.

"I already did," I told her. Then I went into our apartment and went to bed.

CHAPTER 9

I was so tired I couldn't sleep. I lay in the dark listening to the sound of the television. My father was watching an old movie. I thought about Thelma's party, about the twerpy talk about the Riviera. The only good thing that happened was that I'd managed to keep my mouth shut and hadn't let it slip that I thought the Riviera was in New Jersey. Boy, that would've been the end.

How come I never get to go anyplace? How come everyone I know has been somewhere or is going? Polly's a world traveler, due to her father's job. Al's got big, exciting plans to go to the farm, have a barn dance, plus homemade ice cream. Even Teddy gets to go to

Connecticut. Only I sit home. I lead a very boring life, I've decided.

When I woke in the morning, it was raining. I lay with my hands behind my head and listened to the rain slap against the windows. It was cooler already. Good.

"Those guys are certainly into culture," I said aloud. Wait'll I told Polly about last night. I'd write her today.

My father was fixing breakfast when I came into the kitchen. "How come you're not at the office?" I said. "It's late."

"It's also Saturday," he said, expertly flipping his egg. He's not so hot at cooking, but I will say he flips a mean egg.

"It feels like Tuesday," I said.

"Suppose we splurge tonight and go out to dinner. How would that be?" my father said.

"Oh, Dad!" I hugged him. "That would be super. Just you and me. Wonderful! Just for that, I'll clean the house before Mom comes home."

"That'd be nice. And I'll do the marketing. What do we need?"

"Everything," I told him. "Milk, butter, eggs, meat, veggies. But if we're going out tonight, you don't have to buy stuff until tomorrow. The stores stay open on Sunday half day, I think."

After I ate and got dressed, I decided to go over to Al's. I'd write to Polly later.

"I'm over at Al's if you want me," I said. My father

was concentrating so hard on making out the shopping list I wasn't sure he'd heard me. I opened the door and turned around.

"I'm at Al's, Dad," I said again.

He looked up. "I thought Al was off and running to the bucolic fleshpots," he said. That's the way he talks sometimes. He gets it from *his* father. I'm used to it. You have to know what "bucolic" means, not to mention "fleshpots." In our family we use the dictionary a lot. I'm always amazed at how much my father hears. He appears to be a man who lives in his own world. He also is hard-of-hearing. That's what he says, but I've noticed he hears what he wants to. I hadn't been sure he even knew Al was going to the farm.

"She leaves Wednesday," I said. "For three weeks."

"Um. Well, you'll miss her, I know. Tell her for me I hope she has a bon voyage. I bet she's excited."

"She is," I said. Until that minute I hadn't realized how much I would miss Al. When my father said that, it hit me. I'd miss her like mad. Three weeks was a long time to be gone. One time Al had said something about asking her father and Louise if I could go with her to the farm. But she'd never mentioned it again. I knew she couldn't take a perfect stranger there. Still, I kept hoping she'd bring it up again. But she hadn't, and I knew, in my secret heart, she wouldn't. Polly was still at the Cape. That left me. My two best friends would be gone. Boy.

"Dad, do you think we could afford to go on a vacation this year?" I asked.

58

"It doesn't look promising," my father said.

One thing about my father, he didn't say, "We'll see." If there's anything I hate, it's when grown-ups say, "We'll see."

I rang Al's bell. Every time I do that I'm glad we live so close. It's great to be able to zap down the hall and ring your best friend's bell.

She opened the door. She had on her Peanuts pajamas. She says she knows she's too old to wear Peanuts pajamas, but she does, anyway.

"My mother's sick," she said. "I'm taking her to the doctor." Her voice was different, dull and so low it was hard to hear.

"What?" I said. "The doctor?"

"I called him and he said to bring her over. He can't come out to see her. He's too busy. She's getting dressed now."

"What's the matter with her?" I said.

"She's got this cough," Al said.

I nodded. "You told me."

"She coughed all last night. This morning she said she thought she'd stay in bed. So I got scared. She almost never stays home from work. So I called the doctor. And he said, 'Does she have any pain in her chest?' and I asked her if she had any pain in her chest, and she said she had a little. So then the doctor said put her in a cab and bring her right over to his office. So that's what I'm doing."

Her voice didn't change all the time she was talking. It

59

was as if she were reciting words that meant nothing.

"You want me to go with you?" I said. "My father could go, if you want."

Al shook her head. "No, thanks," she said. "I can manage." And slowly, softly, the door started to close, until it was only open a crack.

"You're sure?" I said to Al's eye, which was all I could see of her. "If you need anything, I'm here."

"Thanks," I heard her say. Then the crack disappeared and she went with it.

CHAPTER 10

"You better go with her, Dad," I told my father. "She said she didn't need any help, but I think you ought to at least offer."

I listened as my father dialed Al's number and talked to her. He offered his services, said he'd be glad to accompany her and her mother to the doctor. She told him the same thing she told me. "I can manage," she said over the phone. I heard her. "Thank you anyway, but I can manage."

"Well," my father told her, "we'll be here if you need us, Al." Then he hung up.

"I've done all I could do," he said. "If she doesn't

want anyone to go along, you certainly can't force yourself on them. Al will manage. At least she's seeing that her mother gets to the doctor. That's the important thing." Then he went to the store to do the marketing.

I sat down and tried to write a letter to Polly. I tried to make the letter funny, to make Polly laugh as I wrote about last night at Thelma's. I had to be careful, though. Polly and Thelma were friends. I didn't want to make too much fun of Thelma. Polly wouldn't like it if I did. I told about the other kids and how all they talked about was how they were going to make big bucks when they grew up. And I also told her about the conversation about the Riviera and what Al had said about the handkerchief tucked into the armpit. That would give Polly a good laugh.

Every time I heard a noise in the hall, I got up and listened at the door. Once or twice I opened the door. The hall was always empty. Time passed very slowly. Every time I checked the clock, only a few minutes had gone by. I went back to my letter writing. I told Polly about going to Tiffany's, leaving out the part about what Al said about maybe marrying Brian and living off the land. I told her about the zoo. I'd make Polly sorry she was missing all the fun here at home. Temperature 85, humidity 90 percent. She only thought she was having a blast going sailing and swimming every day. What did she know?

My wastebasket filled up gradually with balls of paper

I'd thrown away. Letter writing is not the easiest thing in the world. At last I heard the elevator door opening. I rushed to the door. My father stood there, juggling two big bags of groceries, trying to hit the doorbell with his elbow. I let him in.

"Would you believe this little bit of food cost me more than fifty dollars?" he said. It does men good to do the marketing, my mother says. That's the only way they're going to learn about the high cost of living. I helped him unpack the stuff. I kept going to the door and listening. Maybe I could help when Al and her mother got home. Probably the doctor would give Al's mother some medicine to fix her up. Al might have to go to the drugstore to get a prescription filled. I could sit with her mother while she went.

The minutes dragged by. My father said it had stopped raining. He went out to do some errands, pick up some things at the dry cleaner's. I thought if Al didn't get home soon, I'd split a gut. It had been more than two hours, now, since she'd left. Usually doctors keep you waiting in the office. That's why they have so many magazines for patients to read. I hoped he wouldn't keep Al's mother waiting too long.

On the other hand, maybe Al would call me from her apartment. Instead of ringing the bell, that is. I hate waiting for the telephone to ring. The suspense is terrible. To keep myself busy, I put clean sheets on the beds. Not Teddy's. He wouldn't know a clean sheet if it hit him in the face. Just my parents' bed and mine. The phone still hadn't rung. I made us some deviled ham for sandwiches for lunch. I jazzed it up with pickle relish and some chopped egg. My father would never recognize that deviled ham.

Our apartment is at the back of the building. Even if I wanted to, I couldn't see Al and her mother when their taxi pulled up in front. They'd have to take a taxi if Al's mother was sick. Al said her mother wouldn't take a taxi even in a blizzard and if she had a broken leg. This time she'd have to.

Still no Al. I was tempted to go out for a walk. But sure as shooting, if I did that, the minute my back was turned, Al would come home and might need me for something. Maybe just to talk to. I stayed put.

When I'd about given up, I heard the elevator door slide open. I looked out. It was Al. She was alone.

She looked at me. I didn't say anything. She wasn't sucking in her cheeks or anything, the way she does when she wants to look older. But still, she looked older.

She came inside. I figured I wouldn't ask her any questions until she felt like talking.

"You took so long," I said at last.

"I know." Al began to pace the room. Around and around she went, like a dog settling down for a nap.

"She had to go to the hospital," Al said. She cleared her throat. "The doctor said she'd be better off there. I guess he's right. It's nothing serious, he says. It's pneumonia. But not serious, he said." She looked at me, and her eyes were filled with fear.

"I mean," she said, "it's not as if she was going to die or anything."

Al resumed her pacing. I didn't know what to do. I was tempted to pace with her. Anything to keep us both busy. My father came home. He was loaded with packages, and several cleaner's plastic bags dangled from one hand.

"Hi, Dad!" I shouted, as if he'd been away on a trip and I hadn't seen him for ages. Even to my own ears, my voice sounded phony.

"Oh, hello, Al. Everything go all right?" my father asked in a cheery voice. "Get your mother fixed up?"

Al stood on a corner of the rug, looking at us. Her

hands hung at her sides. Her face looked smooth, empty. Behind her glasses, her eyes were dull.

"The doctor says Al's mother has to go to the hospital," I told my father. "She has pneumonia. She's already there. In the hospital. It's nothing serious, the doctor says."

The three of us stood there. Even my father seemed undecided as to what to do or say. And he was grown up.

"Well," he said at last, "they clear up pneumonia very quickly these days. With the right drug. You'll stay with us then, Al, until your mother is well."

I have always loved my father. But never as much as I did at that moment. He had said exactly the right thing.

Al's face brightened. "Thanks," she said. "I don't know. I have to be near the telephone. The doctor said he'd call me about five to let me know how she was doing. He said not to come back to the hospital until tomorrow. He said he'd start treatment immediately. He said she needs rest, lots of rest. But he said he'd call me and let me know how she was doing."

"Help me with these things, will you?" We rushed to my father's aid.

"I tell you what you do, Al," he said. "Call the doctor's office and give them our number. Then you won't have to worry about missing his call. Why don't you go home now and get what you need. I'll be here. If he should call while you're gone, I'll come down to your place and let you know."

My father had taken charge. It was wonderful. That's what Al needed more than anything else. Someone to tell her what she should do.

I went with her. Her apartment was clean and calm. It had a different smell from ours. I'm very aware of the way places smell. Hers smelled of her mother. Our apartment smells of my mother, but also of Teddy and my father. And me. Every person has their own individual smell. Al's mother uses lots of bath oil and moisturizer. And perfume. Al's mother is big on perfume. Also on staying moist. Being in Better Dresses is not easy, as Al tells me from time to time.

Al stuffed her pajamas and toothbrush into her knapsack. Her suitcase sat on the bed. On top was the lavender sweater her mother had given her. Neither of us looked at it. We pretended it wasn't there.

She called the doctor's office and left our number with the receptionist. Then she looked around. "I guess that's it," she said. "Oh, one more thing. I better make my mother's bed. She hates her room to be messy."

Together we went into Al's mother's room. It was a pretty room, with flowered sheets and pale, soft colors. We made the bed and Al put away a pair of shoes that lay disconsolately on the rug. Those shoes looked abandoned, like people waiting at a bus stop. I don't know why it is, but people waiting at a bus stop always seem to look sad. And tired. And abandoned, as if they were waiting for someone who might never come. First, Al tossed the shoes carelessly into the closet. Then she went back and picked them up, brushed them off and put shoe trees in them so they'd keep their shape.

"My mother's very particular about taking care of her stuff," Al told me proudly. "She says if you take good care of your things, they last a lifetime. Whatever a lifetime is." Her shoulders drooped, as if they were weighed down with something invisible.

For good luck, we punched up the pillows on the bed so they swelled to twice their size.

"Now everything's ready for when she gets back." Al looked around. Her fingers started twisting her hair into a knot.

"O.K.," she said. "Let's go. The doctor's calling me in a little while. At your place."

"We better get back then," I said. "In case he's calling right this minute." I wanted to get home. I wanted to leave Al's apartment. It felt sad, deserted. We left Al's mother's room and zapped down the hall, fast. So we wouldn't miss the doctor's call.

I guessed my father and I wouldn't be going out to dinner after all. Not tonight, anyway. Not with Al staying with us.

I'd never been out to dinner with just my father before.

CHAPTER 12

The doctor called almost on the stroke of five, as he'd promised. Thank God. There's nothing worse than waiting for a phone call that doesn't come. Especially when it's from a doctor. He told Al her mother was resting comfortably and that she could have visitors tomorrow. Between two and four.

"Don't stay long," he warned. "Five or ten minutes at the most. Your mother's tired. The important thing is plenty of rest. She's pretty run-down."

When she hung up, Al repeated what the doctor had said. "I kept telling her she should get to bed earlier," Al said. "But she wouldn't listen to me."

Then my mother called from Connecticut to say she and Teddy would be home tomorrow evening. "It's been lovely," she said. "We've had a wonderful time. But it will be nice to get home. I've missed you. Have you eaten anything but hamburger? I bet the house is a mess."

I told her the house wasn't a mess and that Al was staying with us due to the fact that her mother was in the hospital with pneumonia. My mother said she was sorry to hear that. "I'm glad you're looking out for Al. Don't forget to give her clean towels," my mother said. She has a clean towel fetish. Also a fetish about us eating nothing but hamburger. I ignored that remark. She sometimes thinks she knows everything we do, my mother.

I got out some towels and arranged them carefully on the towel rack. "You don't have to go to all that trouble," Al said. "I could use a corner of yours."

My father peered around the corner of the bathroom door. "Pull yourselves together, girls. I made a reservation for six-thirty."

"We're going out?" I said, surprised. "Al's here, Dad," I reminded him. I didn't think he could afford to take both Al and me out for dinner.

"I know she is. I've got myself all set for some thinly sliced cucumbers covered with sour cream into which has been snipped some fresh dill," my father said, smacking his lips. "Get a move on."

Al's eyes were huge. "I'm going out to dinner with you and your father," she said softly. "I can't stand it. I simply cannot stand it." She zapped toward the door.

"Where are you going?" I called to her.

"Home. To change," she said. "I'll be back in a flash."

I had planned on wearing my new jeans and a clean T-shirt. Now I'd have to change into my dress, the dress my mother had bought me to wear to church on Easter. My only dress. Probably Al would wear the dress she had bought to wear to her father's wedding. I hadn't worn mine since Easter. It was blue with flowers on it.

"Smashing," my father said when he saw me. "You look ravishing." He looked at my feet. "You think those sneakers do justice to the rest of you?" I went back and struggled into my shoes. They felt tight. When you're accustomed to wearing sneakers, shoes always feel tight. I guessed I could stand tight shoes for one night.

When Al returned, she was breathing hard. Sure enough, she had on the red-and-white check dress her mother had bought her to go with the red shoes with the clunky heels she'd worn to the wedding. The dress was a little tight around the waist, Al said. "I'm going to have to take it easy tonight or it might give way," she confided to me. "Just as well. I don't want your father to rack up a big bill at the restaurant on my account."

"With all this youth and beauty I certainly hope I run into someone I know," my father told us. Al's cheeks got bright red. On the way down in the elevator she kept giving me and my father piercers, as if to make sure this was really happening to her, that it wasn't a dream. She got off the elevator first so I could tell her if her behind wiggled. I told her no, although I thought I detected a tiny trace of a wiggle. It was the shoes. They made her wiggle. But I didn't tell Al that. I knew it would spoil her evening. Besides, no one but me would notice.

My father took us to a French restaurant called La Bonne Femme. There were flowers on the table and linen napkins also. That's a true sign of a classy restaurant: flowers plus linen napkins. I slid a glance over to Al to make sure she was taking everything in. She was.

The waiter pulled out both our chairs with a flourish. He had a terrific mustache, thick and curly, and big brown eyes. His teeth were beautiful and white. He looked more like a rock star than a waiter. He flirted a little bit with Al and me. Probably he thought he'd get a bigger tip if he did. I didn't mind. Al pretended she wasn't aware of him, but I knew she was. I was glad I'd changed into my shoes.

"Would mademoiselle like to try the pâté?" the waiter said. He was talking to both of us.

"Yes, please," I said. Al frowned at the menu, probably checking out the prices. "I'll have the pâté too," she said. My father had vichyssoise. They didn't have cucumbers with freshly snipped dill on the menu.

"The sole véronique is superb tonight," the waiter whispered to us, his eyes sparkling, his mustache quivering. "Superb."

We both chose that. My father said he'd like the boeuf

en daube. When the waiter had gone, I said, "What's 'véronique' mean?" My father said, "With grapes." Al nodded as if she'd known that all along. She sat with her hands folded primly in her lap, not missing a trick. Me too. One of the things I love best about going to a restaurant to dinner is the people. Watching them is half the fun. And catching snatches of conversation is fun too. My mother does that. Eavesdropping, some call it. I glanced over at the next table.

"Hi!" a voice said. "I thought it was you." It was the girl from school who'd gone skiing with her father and his girl friend.

"Oh, hi," I said. Al didn't know her. She was in my science class and Al wasn't. I checked the girl friend. She looked about twenty-one. Probably she was. My friend had told me that since her mother and father got divorced, her father had had about ten different girl friends. Each one, she said, was younger than the one before. "Pretty soon he'll latch onto one who's the same age as me," she'd said gloomily. "And that'll be yucky."

My father asked to see the wine list. Boy, he was really going all-out.

"The mademoiselles will have a glass?" the waiter asked, hovering over us and smiling. He was really very cute. Al took a piece of French bread, broke it in half, and daintily buttered it. She took small bites and chewed with her mouth closed. I did the same.

"Don't fill up on bread, ladies," my father said. "Save yourselves for the pièce de résistance."

While my father was studying the wine list, I leaned over to Al and said, "He means the sole véronique."

She glared at me and said, "I know that." She didn't like for me to imply her French wasn't as good as mine. I could feel my school friend at the next table watching us—me and my father and Al. Then our pâté came. It had tiny pickles on the plate with it—*cornichons,* they call them. They were sour. I saw Al's hand go toward the bread basket, then pull back. After every bite we both patted our lips genteelly with our napkins. We were going all-out too. Once it crossed my mind that I would've liked it better if I'd been alone with my father. Just once. Then I felt ashamed of myself. I knew how much Al was enjoying herself. That was selfish of me, to want my father all to myself. But I couldn't help it.

"This beats hamburgers and French fries, right?" my father said when the waiter cleared our plates and we waited for our entrées. I bet if it was just my father and me, we'd go out to a restaurant about six nights out of the week. It seemed to me that the whole room glowed. The sole was sensational.

"I have never had a better dinner," Al told my father. "Never." She went out to restaurants a lot. With her mother's beaux. That's what her mother called the men she went out with: beaux. If Al called them boyfriends, her mother really freaked out.

"My compliments to the chef," my father said to the waiter. Just like in the movies.

It was the kind of restaurant where they had a dessert

tray. They pushed this little cart around to your table, and on it were bowls of whipped cream, fresh strawberries, éclairs, peach tarts—so many things, and each one of them looked better than the other. Al rested her chin in her hands and gazed at the desserts for a long while. She kept letting out these gigantic sighs.

"I know what I'm having," I said. "Profiterole." That's a cream puff stuffed with ice cream and covered with chocolate sauce. My father said he'd have a piece of cheese and some crackers.

Al looked at him as if he were crazy. "For dessert?" she said. While she was trying to make up her mind, I excused myself to go to the ladies' room. I needed to stretch my legs before dessert. Also, I like to check out ladies' rooms. There are ones that have saucers in which rests a quarter or two. That means you're supposed to add some money to them. Usually there's an attendant to hand you a towel if you wash your hands. This was a no-saucer-type ladies' room, I'm happy to say. I leaned down to check the booths. No feet. I was alone.

The door opened. It was my friend from school.

"How come I never saw you here before?" she said. "That kid with you is Al, right? We come here all the time."

"Oh, we go lots of different places," I said, fluttering my eyelashes. "My father likes to go different places. He gets bored going to the same restaurant all the time." There is one thing about lying: the more you do it, the better you get, the easier the words slip out. This is sad but true.

The kid washed her hands and stuck out her chin until it almost touched the mirror.

"I'm getting zits," she said.

"Is that Clorinda?" I asked.

"Who?"

"Your father's girl friend Clorinda. The one who twisted her ankle when you went skiing?"

"Heck, no. This one's name is Taffy. Is that dumb or is that dumb?" She screwed up her face. "Is that your father?"

"Yes," I said.

"Where's your mother? I thought you said they were still married." She gave me a watered-down version of a piercer. Nowhere near as good as Al's.

"My mother's in Connecticut." When I lied, it sounded like the truth. When I told the truth, it sounded like a lie. I don't think she believed me. She probably thought my mother was off getting a divorce somewhere.

"Oh, well." She sighed. "I better get back. They need me for relief. I play the straight man. They bounce their ideas off me. See you."

As she went out, Al came in. "Where were you?" she said. "I thought you drowned. Who was that?"

"She's in my science class," I said. "She's with her father and his girl friend. Her name's Taffy."

"That's a dumb name," Al said.

"That's the girl friend's name. My friend's name is Mary."

Al went to the bathroom. When she came out, she washed her hands. "I was going to offer to pay for my dinner," she said. "I brought some money and stuffed it under my pillow at your house. Then I thought your father might be insulted. If I did that, I mean. What do you think?"

"I think he'd have a fit," I said. "He wanted you to come. You're his guest."

"It's a neat restaurant," Al said. "It's the nicest one I've ever been to. Your father is a terrific man. He's practically the nicest man I know. Outside of my own father, that is."

We went back to the table. The dessert was sitting there, waiting for us. Al had chosen strawberry shortcake. The reason I know is that she told me. I wouldn't have been able to identify it. There was so much whipped cream on top that you couldn't see the strawberries. As we ate, my father watched us. Al ate each bite slowly, lingering over every mouthful of whipped cream. I couldn't finish my profiterole. I never can. I always think this time I might, and then I feel a little sick and have to leave some.

"Mademoiselle's eyes are bigger than her stomach," the waiter said, flashing his eyes and his teeth at me. I don't think he was French at all. Still, he was cute. He was probably an out-of-work actor. Lots of waiters in

New York are out-of-work actors. Someday he might be a star.

Too bad they can't put ice cream in a doggie bag.

My father paid the check. He left a big tip. He always does. Then he suggested we go to a movie. We said no, thank you. I didn't want him to spend any more money.

"It was wonderful," I said. "Thanks, Dad."

Al shook his hand. "Thank you a thousand times," she said. "I never had a better time in my whole life."

My father shook her hand back. "It wouldn't have been as nice without you, Al," he said. My father is a good man.

After we went to bed, I heard Al tossing and turning. I thought about tonight. If my father and I went out to dinner all the time, it wouldn't be nearly as special. Like being alone, going out to dinner was a rare treat. If it happened all the time, the bloom would be off the rose. I decided once in a while was super. I didn't want to get too used to the good things in life.

Al's voice said, "Do you realize I never thought about my mother once tonight? The whole entire time we're living it up in the restaurant, I never thought about her once?" She sounded on the verge of tears. "How do you like that?"

Then she said, "You were pretty neat, letting me come along. I know you would've liked it better if it was just you and your father. But you made room for me. That was very nice of you. Thank you."

I breathed long, regular breaths so Al would think I was asleep. For some reason, I didn't want her to know I'd heard what she said. I don't know why, I just didn't. But I was glad she'd said it.

The next day we walked up First Avenue to the hospital. Through the thick, hot Sunday silence, a heat so dense it seemed to muffle sounds, we walked, not talking much. As we stepped off the curb at Sixty-fifth Street, a huge black limousine turned the corner and bore down on us. As if we weren't there. That car was so gigantic it resembled a family-size hearse. The guy behind the wheel was probably used to having pedestrians flee from him. When you're that big, that powerful, that intimidating, you must get accustomed to having obstacles in your path dissolve. We were supposed to dissolve.

Al perked up. That car had the same effect on her that

Martha Moseley usually does. Even when she's in the pits, if Martha crosses her path, she livens up considerably. I could almost see her adrenaline churning through her veins, reviving, restoring, renewing her.

"Not today, bud," she said, and held her arm out, stiff as a ramrod, like a traffic cop telling traffic to cease and desist while he helps a little old lady across the street.

We kept on going. The limo kept on coming. One of us was going to have to give in. I was all for it. I liked being in one piece. Not Al. She had made up her mind he wasn't going to steamroll over us. She knew her rights. I knew if I turned and wimped my way back and stood on the sidewalk with my thumb in my mouth or something, waiting for the limo to go on its merry way, she'd never forgive me. I stuck by her, but my teeth were chattering. No mean feat in New York City in July.

The windows of the car were all tightly shut. That meant it was air conditioned. Probably the fat cats inside were discussing multimillion-dollar deals. The windows were the dark, fogged-up kind, the kind we couldn't see through but the people inside could see out of. Rock musicians have cars with windows like that. So do TV personalities. So people won't stare in at them, I guess.

"Maybe it's a corporation president in there," Al suggested. "Excuse me, sir"—she raised her voice—"but are you a corporation president?"

The driver stared at us. He looked dead. Maybe he was. He wore a chauffeur's cap, and his face was made of stone. He also wore dark glasses. He took his hand off the wheel and made an obscene gesture. The diamond ring on his pinky caught the light and winked at us. I wouldn't have been surprised to see a submachine gun pointed at me. I had everything I could do to keep from running. It seemed to me I could feel the car's bumper against my leg.

"Hurry," I whispered. "Let's move."

Al came to a halt, blocking the car's way. She did a couple of bumps and grinds for good measure, smiling at the driver. I stayed behind her as best I could. This time it was me using her for a shield. Then slowly, like a couple of snails on their way to the dentist, we inched our way to the opposite curb. And stood there, triumphant, as the driver gunned the motor like he was in training for the Daytona 500, making a lot of noise to show us he was the big macho macho guy he'd always been.

"Please, God," Al said softly, "let him stall. Please. That isn't too much to ask, is it?" I guess it was. Smoothly, like a gigantic black snake, the big black car slithered its way down the block. I checked the rear windows, hoping to see a face looking out at us. There was no one.

A man standing in front of O'Malley's Saloon picked his teeth and regarded us with some interest.

"That's one for the home team, huh?" he said.

"You bet," Al agreed. I smiled at the man. He lifted his shoulders and returned to the dark depths of O'Malley's.

We continued on our way. Al was much more cheerful. That kind of encounter, the good guys against the bad guys, always cheered her. But by the time we reached the hospital, she was quiet again. I sat down in one of the phony leather chairs they had in the waiting room and opened my paperback. I watched as Al went up to the desk, and after a bit the woman behind it handed her a card. Then Al went over to the elevators. I pretended to be reading. When I looked up, she was gone.

Someone sat down beside me. It was a man. Out of the corner of my eye I saw his hands. He had a handkerchief balled up in his hand. He worked that poor handkerchief around the head and shoulders: he balled it up, then stretched it out on his knee and smoothed it over and over, then balled it up again. Then he got up and walked away. I think he was waiting for something terrible to happen. I never saw his face, but that's what I think. I watched him walk out of the main door. I didn't see him again.

Al came down. We started home. I waited for her to tell me about her mother. She walked very fast.

"Slow down," I said, huffing and puffing. "Slow down, can't you?"

She slowed but not much.

"How is she?" I asked at last.

"She's all right," Al said. "The doctor came in while I was there, and he said she was coming along fine."

"That's good," I said. I wondered why she seemed so

glum. "I think that's very good news. Don't you?"

"Sure. It's terrific." She stomped along.

"Did he say when she could come home?" I asked.

"He said he'd know better tomorrow. He did some tests and took some X-rays, he said, and he'd get the results tomorrow."

Tomorrow. Two days after tomorrow Al was supposed to go to the farm. The day after that was the barn dance.

"Oh," I said. Together we sped home. I had a terrible pain in my side when we pulled up in front of our apartment building. We took the elevator up to our floor.

"My mother should be home soon," I said. "And Teddy."

Al fumbled at her front, to get her front door key. "You're coming to our place, aren't you?" I said, surprised.

"Oh, not tonight, with your mother and Teddy coming home and all," she said. "I thought I'd bunk in alone tonight. Maybe tomorrow I'll come over. I don't want to wear out my welcome." She attempted a smile, which didn't really succeed.

"Don't be a dope," I said. "My mother will have a cow if you don't sleep over at our house. Until your mother comes home."

"Well," Al said, "I don't want to be in the way or anything."

"You would never be in the way," I told her. "You're like a member of our family."

"I am?" Al said, startled. "Really?"

"Sure. Come on in and stop being silly." I opened our door. "Besides, I need a helping hand. There's a lot of picking up to be done before they get here."

"A lot of picking up or a lot of shoveling out?" Al said in a jaunty way.

"You name it, we've got it," I said.

CHAPTER 14

"I hear them!" I cried, and ran to open the door. My mother was standing there, smiling at me. Until that moment I hadn't realized how much I'd missed her.

"Mom! Welcome home!" I hugged her, she hugged me. Then she spied Al behind me and gave her a big hug too. My father came out to greet her, and they went into a clinch that lasted for about sixty seconds. We stood and watched. They didn't even know we were there.

"Wow," I heard Al say under her breath. Teddy scuttled in, bowed down by the weight of his rucksack that made him look as if he were about to scale Mount Rainier.

"Hey, wimp," I said, "you look as if you'd shrunk."

"How'd it go, Ted?" Al asked. "You catch any rattlers or pythons up there in darkest Connecticut?"

Teddy shot us a dark look. "Lots of stuff going on up there I can't talk about," he said. "Lots," and he trudged off to his room, bent almost double.

"What's he got in that thing—rocks?" Al said.

"I wonder if Teddy's mixed up with the Mafia or the C.I.A.?" I said. We went into the kitchen to see to dinner so my mother wouldn't have to lift a finger her first night home. She looked great—rested, tan. "You look cute, Mom," I told her. She'd had her hair cut while she was away. It was very short and curled around her face. My mother is a very attractive woman, if I do say so.

"That haircut makes you look about fifteen," my father told her, smiling.

"She doesn't look any fifteen to me," Teddy said, chewing with his mouth open. I always think I should miss Teddy more. I try to. I try to imagine what life would be without him. Once I read a story about two brothers, and one of them died, and how bad the other one felt. It brought tears to my eyes. I made a promise then and there to never be mean to Teddy again. To cherish him and love him. But every time I saw him chewing with his mouth open, all my promises were broken. I felt bad about those broken promises but figured they were Teddy's fault, not mine. If he hadn't been so repulsive, he would've been a lot easier to cherish.

My mother asked Al a little about her mother, how she was, what the doctor had said. "We're going to the hospital tomorrow to see her," I told my mother. "I'm going too."

We cleared the dishes off while my mother and father had coffee. I made Teddy help load the dishwasher. He likes to stand and hurl plates and glasses into it from as far away as possible. He figures if he smashes enough stuff, he won't be asked to load it again. I told him to clean up his act or I'd break both his legs. He shaped up a little but not much.

"Bath time," my mother said, yawning. "I'm tired," she said. So she and my father excused themselves and went into their bedroom to watch TV. I told Teddy to take a bath and that I'd call Dad if he gave me any trouble. Then he was in there for so long, not making a sound, I thought maybe he'd drowned. All he was doing was making surface dives to explore the bottom of the bathtub.

"Look at this place!" I hollered. "I just cleaned it yesterday! Now look at it." I made him dry himself and scrub out the tub and mop up the floor. By the time he'd finished, he was glassy-eyed with fatigue and didn't even fight me when I told him to go to bed.

Then Al and I went to bed too and read for a while.

"Maybe tomorrow we can write a joint letter to

Polly," I said. "First you write a paragraph, then me. How about it?"

"O.K.," Al agreed. She turned on her side and pulled up the sheet.

"You going to sleep already?" I said.

"No, I'm just thinking," she said.

"What about?" I asked. She didn't answer so I read another chapter. Then she said in a slow and dreamy way, "If I marry Brian, maybe we could live right down the road from my father and Louise and visit them every Sunday. And they'd ask us to stay for dinner. We'd probably have roast chicken or roast beef with lots of gravy and farm-fresh vegetables. And pie à la mode."

"Boy, if Mr. Richards could hear you planning to pig out like that," I said, "he'd hand you a mess of carrot sticks and tell you to go to it."

"I'd get to know the boys really well," Al went on in the same slow and dreamy voice, "and we'd be a big family. Closely knit, as they say. And if my father and Louise wanted to go to the movies or anything, we could sit with the boys. Then, when we had a family, our own kids, my father and Louise could sit with them."

I put down my book. There was no sense in trying to read when Al was on a life plan kick.

"This wouldn't happen for a long time," she said, turning around to look at me. "Not until I made sure my mother was taken care of. If she marries Mr. Wright or whoever she marries, then she could come visit us too. But I would never just go off and leave my mother. I'd see she was settled down first. She'd have her husband, I'd have Brian." Al lay on her back and smiled up at the ceiling, imagining how it would be.

Boy. One minute we're best friends, my father takes her out to dinner in a fancy restaurant and everything, the next minute she's practically wiping me off the face of the map.

What about living down the hall from each other? What about all the times she was in the pits and I cheered her up? What about knowing Mr. Richards? Now she was getting her mother married off and planning her life with Brian. Just as if I were some wimpy kid whose last name she didn't even know who sat behind her in history and copied her notes.

Just as if I were a casual acquaintance.

Boy.

CHAPTER 15

The next morning we hung around waiting for the doctor to call with the results of the tests on Al's mother.

"Let's write to Polly now," I said.

"I'm no good at writing letters," Al said. She was feeling depressed. I could tell. Al would make a terrible poker player. When she's down, she's down. When she's up, she's up. And her face tells it all. She's never in between.

"I stink as a letter writer." She didn't have to tell me. When she wrote to Brian, she started out with "Brian, old buddy," and finished off, after a ton of gnashing of teeth and pacing, with "Your old pal, Al." Just so he wouldn't get the wrong idea. She wanted him to know that theirs was to be a platonic friendship. Boy, she certainly had changed her tune.

I started. I wrote:

> *Dear Pol—*
>
> *We're having a blast here. Too bad you're up in the land of saltwater and codfish. Poor you. The social season here is picking up. My father took Al and me to a classy restaurant for dinner, and we went to Thelma's for spaghetti. She had two extra boys (twerps), which is why she asked us. And a clone called Daisy. Art and Tommy and Ned talked about making big bucks. Perry couldn't come, due to chicken pox. All those bozos talk about is making money. I think they were midgets in disguise. I'll tell you more when I see you.*

"Now it's your turn," I told Al.

She scratched her head and said, "People like Thelma freak me out. I wonder how come she and a good kid like Polly are friends."

"Stop talking and start writing," I said. "That was the deal."

"Does what I write have to be true or can I fake it?" Al asked.

I thought about that. "Spice it up if you want. I don't

think Polly would care. She needs some excitement, after all. Lolling around on the beach up there, away from civilization."

So Al wrote:

> *Dear Polly—*
>
> *I am going to a nudist camp. It is co-ed. The nudist camp is also a fat farm. I plan on hiding my instamatic camera in my pajamas. We walk around starkers all day and wear pajamas at night on account of the mosquitoes are ferocious. They're as big as hummingbirds. I plan on selling my pics to the* NATIONAL BLAD. *Hope you're not bored where you are. Please answer this letter.*

"That'll grab Polly," I said approvingly. "You write very good letters. You really do."

"I do?" Al looked pleased.

"Sure. If you wrote letters like that to Brian, he'd answer you by return mail. Why don't you write funny stuff like that to him?"

"It's different. When it's a boy, it's different."

"How?"

"I don't know. It just is." Al twisted a strand of her hair around her finger. Around and around she went. She would have an awful time combing it out.

"Do you realize how lucky you are?" she said suddenly. "You're so lucky and you don't even know it."

"Me? Lucky? How come?" I said, surprised.

"You have a family. You're all together, eating, sleeping, watching TV."

"So are you a family. You and your mother," I said.

"A family," Al said, "is more than two people. I checked in the dictionary. A family is a group of people living under one roof. No matter how you slice it"—she smiled a sour smile—"my mother and I are not a group." She started to pace. Then she stopped and wiped off her glasses with her shirttail.

"How about you being lucky?" I said in a too-loud voice. "You're going off on this jazzy trip, going to a barn dance in a real barn, and everything. All I get to do is sit home and wait for you to write to tell me about all the fun you're having. I sit here waiting for summer to end so I can go back to school for some excitement." My voice rose. She was listening to me, though. "I'm not going anywhere. You're the one who's having all the fun. Maybe you ought to stop and think about who's lucky."

We stared at each other. The silence between us grew and grew like weeds in a garden. It filled every nook and cranny of the room. Outside I could hear a taxi horn bleating, like a lost sheep. The crosstown bus snorted its way around the corner.

The telephone rang. I jumped. So did Al. I've never been so glad to hear the telephone in all my life.

"Maybe it's the doctor," Al said.

I got to it first.

"Hi," a familiar voice said. "It's me."

"Where are you, creep!" I shouted.

"I'm home. I got home last night."

"It's Polly!" I cried. "She's home. Get on the kitchen phone. We can both talk to her."

I heard Al pick up the extension. She didn't say anything, but I knew she was there.

"I thought you were staying until next week," I said.

"Nope. Here I am. I have a surprise for you," Polly said.

"You're getting married," I guessed.

"Almost right. I'm engaged. But we can't get married until he unloads his wife and eight kids. Come on over, why don't you? Is Al there?"

I waited. Al didn't make a sound.

"Yeah, she's here. We can't come right this minute. Al has to go see her mother this afternoon."

"Where's her mother?"

"In the hospital. She has pneumonia."

"That's too bad," Polly said.

"Speak up, Al. It's Polly," I said.

"Hi," Al said in a thin, watery voice. That was all she said. "Hi."

"What's your surprise?" I asked Polly.

"I'm cooking you guys a lobster dinner," Polly said excitedly. "I brought them down from the Cape. They're so fresh I can hardly believe it. They're delicious when they're fresh like that. When can you come?"

"I'm not sure," Al said in a monotone.

"Well," I said in a loud, positive voice, "I'll be there. Pronto."

"O.K. I'll expect you both," Polly said. "I have scads of info for you. I met this really cute boy. He didn't ask me out on a date or anything but I thought he was going to. Then it turned out he was eleven years old. Can you believe it? He was the tallest eleven-year-old I ever saw. I've gotta go. My mother's standing over me with a whip." And she hung up. I did too. I sat and waited for Al to come out of the kitchen.

"You go," she said. "If I went, I'd put a damper on things. The way I feel now, I'd be a real drag."

"Why don't you wait until after you've seen your mother," I said, "and talked to the doctor. Then you'll feel better."

Al cast a dark look in my direction. "I doubt it," she said. "I have serious doubts that I will feel better."

Sometimes I think that Al likes to wallow in her emotions. I really do.

Al kept pacing, waiting for the doctor to call. I decided to give myself a facial. That way I'd improve my appearance, clear my clogged pores, and hide under a towel to keep the steam in and Al's pacing out. The trouble with a facial, though, is that I always seem to look the same after. Sometimes I look worse.

I ran hot water in the basin and leaned over with the towel draped over my head. Nothing worthwhile is easy, I told myself. Al passed the bathroom. I heard her. I also heard her come to a stop. She was watching me. I lifted the towel and checked the mirror for the results.

"Holy Toledo," she said. "Is it catching?" My face

did sort of look as though I had measles.

"This is what is known as a schoolgirl complexion," I said. "Why anyone wants one is beyond me."

Al started to wring her hands. I could almost see the moisture coming from them. "Why doesn't he call?" she wailed. "I bet something's gone wrong. I feel it in my bones. Something terrible has happened. My mother has had a relapse." One thing about Al is she watches a lot of those hospital soap operas. They give her all kinds of ideas.

The telephone rang.

"You answer," Al said. "Please."

I wiped off my face and picked up the phone.

"Hello, dear," a voice said. "Is Alexandra there?"

"It's your mother," I said, handing Al the receiver, not even stopping to ask Al's mother how she was. I figured if she was well enough to use the phone, she was good for a few more years yet.

"Ma!" Al shouted. "How are you?" She listened. I could hear her mother's voice. She sounded fine.

"Yeah. O.K. The blue one? . . . Sure. Top right-hand drawer. . . . O.K. You want anything else? . . . No, I was planning on coming up this afternoon. O.K. See you." She hung up.

"She's feeling fine. Much better. She says she's ready to come home but that the doctor says she has to stay a couple more days."

"Good. That's great, really great," I said. "That way you can go Wednesday . . . go to the farm, I mean . .

and Mr. Wright can bring her home. Or, if he can't, my mother and I can go up and get her if you don't want her to come home alone." I bent over the basin again.

"I'm sorry I said what I said." Al's voice was so low I could hardly hear her. "About you being so lucky and all. I was so full of my own problems I didn't think about you. You not going anywhere, I mean. That was selfish."

"Hey," I said, "here I am envying you and there you are, envying me. That's life, I guess. The grass is always greener on the other side. Or something like that."

Al twisted her hair into a tight knot. "What's the matter now?" I said. "Your mother's getting better, your trip's Wednesday. What the heck's the matter now?"

"I don't think I can go. To the farm, I mean." Al turned to face me, her eyes huge behind her glasses.

"Why not? Everything's hunky-dory. Why can't you go?"

"Because if I did, I'd be walking out on my mother. Even if she is better, she's still in the hospital. Somebody has to take care of her when she gets home."

"How about Mr. Wright?" I said.

"He's not her family," Al said angrily. "She's not his responsibility. She's mine. Besides, and this is what gets me, you know perfectly well if it was me that was sick she wouldn't walk out on me. So how can I do that to her? Answer me that. How can I?"

I thought for a while. I knew she was right. Still, there was that barn dance and Brian and the three little boys and the homemade ice cream waiting there. Maybe her whole future was waiting for her on the farm.

"I can't," she said. "Can I?"

"Well"—I chose my words very carefully this time—"I don't think you'd have a very good time. I mean, think of all the time you'd be thinking about your mother in the hospital. You'd probably have a super attack of the guilties, don't you think?"

She nodded. "Guilt is a terrible thing. Guilt feelings do a lot of harm. People are always feeling guilty about something. I've read a lot about it. Guilt is very big these days. If you don't feel guilty about something, you're not really trying. For instance." Al sat down. She was getting ready for a dissertation on guilt. When she sits down and locks her ankles like that, she means business.

"I've often wondered if my father suffers from guilt. Because he didn't write to me for such a long time. Someday I'm going to ask him. Just sock it to him, say, 'Dad'—I'm going to say"—Al gave me a piercer to show me how she was going to nail her father—" 'Dad, do you ever have guilt feelings about ignoring me for so long? Do you ever lie awake at night and feel guilty that you left me in the lurch?' What do you think if I do that?"

"I think you'd probably make your father feel terrible," I said. "At least he patched things up and now everything's hunky-dory between you. You might spoil that if you asked him if he felt guilty about you. That's what I think. I think you should let well enough alone."

Al jumped up. She was smiling.

"You are right, O Skinny One," she said. "Not for

the first time and I certainly hope not for the last. You are wise beyond your years. Now I'm going to whip up to the hospital and take my mother a bed jacket she wants. You want to come?"

I said no, I thought I'd stay home. "Tell your mother hello for me," I said. "I'll send her a funny get-well card."

"Good," Al said. "I won't be long. Then we can go over to Polly's." She went to the door. With her hand on the doorknob, she turned and said to me, "That's when I knew my mother would pull through. When she said she wanted a bed jacket, that's when I knew the crisis had passed. See you," and she was gone.

Boy. One minute she's as low as a snake's belly button. The next she's flying high. I figure my forte is as an advice giver. I'm practically on a par with Ann Landers. Only she gets paid for it and I dish it out for free.

CHAPTER 17

When Al got back from the hospital, she was very subdued. She moved slowly, thoughtfully, her head tilted to one side as if she were listening to something. Or someone. I didn't ask her what she'd decided to do about the farm. I figured she'd tell me when she felt like it.

"Polly said to come the minute you got home," I said.

"I better not go." Al washed her face and combed her hair. Then she changed into clean jeans and a clean T-shirt. "I'm in the pits. Mr. Wright was visiting my mother this afternoon. He's so cheerful," Al said scornfully. "I don't think he realizes how serious pneumonia is. I mean, all kinds of things can go wrong. Just when you're not expecting it. He's so cheerful he depresses me."

I wasn't going to argue with her. "It's not the first time you've been in the pits," I said. "Polly won't mind. Come on. Anyway, Teddy's visiting a friend and my mother and father are going out for dinner so you'd be all alone. Besides, you don't want to miss a lobster dinner at Polly's."

She came with me. I knew she would.

We sat and watched Polly as she zapped around her kitchen. She looked like a small, skinny Julia Child. Polly is very graceful. She sort of skimmed over the floor like a bird wrapped in a huge white apron. She told us not to help her, we'd only be in the way. Which suited me fine. We sat there on the high kitchen stools and told Polly about everything that had happened while she was away. Then she told us a bunch of stories about the weirdos up on the Cape.

"There are more weirdos up there than there are in New York, if you can believe it," Polly said.

I guess both Al and I looked doubtful because Polly said, "It's true. There are. I don't know why, but it's true."

"How's Evelyn?" I said. Evelyn's Polly's twenty-year-old sister who is always living with some guy without being married to him, or thinking of marrying some guy her mother doesn't think is right for her. Polly's mother doesn't think Evelyn is ready for marriage. What I think is that Evelyn probably will never be ready for marriage. It's none of my business, I know, but I'm entitled to my own opinion.

"Evelyn's throwing pots these days," Polly said.

"Who at?" Al said.

"That's what you say when a person is into pottery, making pots," Polly said. "Evelyn's also a vegetarian. She eats mounds of tofu and bean sprouts every day. She's thinking of writing a vegetarian cookbook. I'll say one thing for Evelyn." Polly sighed. "She doesn't let the grass grow under her feet, but she's an eternal child."

Polly went and peered into the lobster pot to see how they were doing.

"How's your mother, Al?" she said.

"Much better, thanks," Al said, smiling.

"When are you leaving? On your trip to the farm?" Polly said.

Talk about timing.

The smile fell off Al's face. I could almost hear it drop. She looked at me.

"I'm not sure." Al said the words slowly, as if reluctant to let them go. "I might not go at all. I can't leave my mother in the lurch."

"Her mother wouldn't do it to her," I said.

Polly nodded. "Good for you, Al," she said. "They're done," and we each got a plate and stood in line for our lobsters.

When we got home, Al said, "You go on in. I'll be over as soon as I call."

"Call who?" I said, although I knew who she meant.

"My father. And Louise. I've stalled around long enough. I'm going to call and tell them I can't come. I've been kidding myself all along, telling myself it would be all right if I went. I can't. I just can't go."

"I thought you said the doctor said she was coming along fine," I said feebly. "Your mother wanted a bed jacket. You said the crisis was over if she wanted a bed jacket."

She turned and looked at me. There were two spots of color high on her cheeks.

"The crisis has just begun," Al said, baring her teeth at me in what passed for a smile. "Besides, what's a lousy old trip and a barn dance anyway?"

She did a very small belly dance, and then her arms fell to her sides. "All it is is my life," she said. And she unlocked her door and slid noiselessly inside.

I went home. I wouldn't have stuck around to hear that phone call for anything. Not for anything in the world.

CHAPTER
18

I opened the door even before Al had a chance to ring.

"What'd they say?" I asked her.

Silently we zapped into my room and shut the door. There was no one around to eavesdrop. It was just better that way.

"I called," Al said slowly. Her eyes looked red. Maybe she'd been crying. Maybe when she was by herself in the apartment that smelled of her mother, she'd cried.

"I called them and told them I couldn't come. I told them my mother was sick and in the hospital and I couldn't leave her alone. And Sam—Sam answered the phone, if you can believe it—Sam kept saying, 'Whazza matta, Al? Whyn't you coming?' That's the way he talks. He's only seven, you know.

" 'Whazza matta, Al? Whyn't you coming?' " she repeated, as if Sam had said something brilliant for a seven-year-old. Sam is Al's favorite. Sam is special, Al says.

"So then my father got on and he wanted to know all about my mother and what the doctor had said and what hospital she was in so they could send her flowers. How do you like that?" Al gave me a piercer. That was a good sign. She only gave piercers when she was herself.

"And you know something?"

I shook my head.

"I think my father still has some feeling left for my mother." Al's eyes were big and round and solemn. The spots of color on her cheeks had disappeared and she was pale. "I think in the deepest recesses of his heart he still cherishes her a little." When I first knew Al she told me her mother and father had a very friendly relationship. Even though they were divorced. The reason they got divorced, Al said, was that her father was a perfectionist.

"Just a little," Al went on. "I don't mean anything romantic, you understand." She stared hard at me. "I don't think that for a minute. I think he and Louise are very much in love with each other. I mean I think he might cherish her a little because she's my mother, if you know what I mean."

I wasn't sure I did, but I didn't let on.

"She was his first love," Al said. "That's something you never forget—your first love."

I almost said, "How do you know?" but I kept my mouth shut.

"It must be nice to be someone's first love." Al got up and went to the bathroom. She does that a lot when she's in the middle of a story. I'm used to it now, but it used to bother me. One thing about Al, she never loses the thread of what she's saying.

"Anyway," she said, coming back, "I gave my father the doctor's name and the hospital room number. He wanted to know what kind of flowers my mother likes. I told him anemones. And you know what he said?"

I shook my head.

"He said, 'Of course. Those red and purple flowers. She always *did* like those.' Well, of course, all I hope is that Louise didn't hear him say that. I mean, she might not like that if she knew my father remembered my mother's favorite flowers. Not that Louise is the jealous type. Because she's not. Still." A little smile played over Al's face, like a gentle breeze over still water.

"Then I talked to Louise. She said they were sorry. They were all so sorry, about my mother and about my not coming right then. She said I should let them know the minute I could come. Then you know what she said?"

I just sat there and didn't even bother to shake my head again.

"She said she knew Brian would be sorry too, when he found out I wasn't coming. Well, I think she was making that up. How'd she know he'd be sorry? But that's what she said. How could she know he'd be sorry when she hadn't even told him yet?" Al stopped talking. I think she wanted me to give her an argument. Or to reassure her. Something. I sat there. I'm a good listener.

"So then," Al said, "Louise said they could always have another barn dance. I asked her if they'd made the homemade ice cream yet, and she said no. I'm not sure she was telling me the truth. I think they probably have a freezer full of homemade strawberry ice cream right this minute. She just didn't want me to feel bad. Any worse than I do already, that is.

"Then you know what she said?" Al's voice trembled.

"No," I said.

Al lowered her head and smiled sadly at her feet.

"She said she would pray for my mother." Al looked up at me, and her face was very serious. Behind her glasses her eyes glinted. They looked almost as if they were made of glass. She got up and went into the bathroom again. She stayed there quite a long time. I was beginning to get worried. I thought maybe I ought to see if she was all right. Then she came out.

"Nobody ever said that before," Al went on, as if our conversation hadn't been interrupted. "That they'd pray for my mother, I mean. I thought that was sweet of Louise to say that. She doesn't even know my mother. It's one thing to pray for someone you know," Al said sternly. "It's quite another to pray for someone you don't know. Someone who was your husband's first wife. Someone who is the mother of your stepdaughter. That's what I am, Louise's stepdaughter. Did you realize that? Isn't that amazing?"

Al glanced at me and quickly glanced away.

"Of course, I don't think my mother *needs* prayers said for her. I mean, she's not *that* sick. She's practically well. Still, I guess they can't do any harm. You never know. She could have a relapse."

Al wound down. She stopped talking and sank back on my bed. It had been a weird day, in more ways than one.

CHAPTER 19

"So. How you two dudes doing anyhow?" Teddy said. "What's happening?"

Al and I looked at each other. She was making a list of things her mother wanted her to bring to the hospital this afternoon. Al asked me to go with her. She said probably Mr. Wright would be there, and she didn't want to go alone. "Maybe you'll make him less cheerful," she told me. I didn't quite know how to take that, so I let it alone.

"Get him," Al said to me.

"Don't give me no flak," Teddy growled. "I'm not taking no flak from nobody."

"Ted, when you left," Al said, "you were a sweet, lovely nine-year-old kid. Now you're making like a Kung Fu expert. What happened?"

Teddy grinned. He was delighted at the attention. He feeds on attention. In order to keep the kid in line, it's best to keep a foot firmly in the middle of Teddy's back.

"You talk that way in front of Mom and Dad?" I said.

"That's the way the kids up in Connecticut talk," he said. "They talk tough. They say, 'Don't give me no flak.' They say other stuff I can't tell you, though." He gave us a dark look.

"What's 'flak' mean?" Al asked.

"Who cares? It's the way you say things that counts. There's this kid named Mike. He lives next door in Connecticut. He's older—about fourteen, I think. He gets into a lot of trouble. The police are always coming to Mike's house," Teddy announced, full of pride. "He rips stuff off from the five-and-ten. Then once he put sugar in a guy's gas tank. If you put sugar in a gas tank, the car won't go. Bet you didn't know that!" Teddy crowed.

"Sounds like you got home just in time, Ted," Al said. "You might've landed in the pokey yourself."

"It just so happened that when Mike was putting sugar in the gas tank," Teddy went on, "the guy who owned the car was looking out the window and saw him. So the police car pulled up in front of Mike's house one more time," he ended with relish. He grinned at us as if he'd been the one who'd put the sugar in the gas tank. "There's lots more things Mike did," Teddy said. "Lots more I could tell you."

Al put her hand over her heart. "Spare me," she said. "She said to bring stationery, because she has lots of thank-you letters to write," she told me. "Your mother and father sent her some beautiful flowers. One reason I want you to come with me today is that my mother wants to see you. To thank you."

"For what?" Teddy said.

"For having me here," Al said.

Teddy squinted at her. "You staying here?" he said. "You sleeping over?" His narrow face was sharp and watchful. Teddy keeps score on how many friends I have to sleep over versus how many he has. He thinks I have more. He's right. But I'm older.

"Yes," Al said. "I'm sleeping over." She sounded sad.

"How long?" Teddy said.

"I don't know. Maybe a few more nights."

He turned to me. "I thought she was going to the farm," he said accusingly.

"Did she say she wanted bath powder?" I said hurriedly. "Or was it face powder?"

"Aren't you going to the farm, Al?" Teddy, once wound up, is hard to stop. "That's what you told me. You said you were going to a barn dance and have homemade ice cream and . . ."

The kid can hardly remember his own name most days.

"Shut up," I told him.

Teddy looked hurt. "She told me that. I didn't make it up. Did I, Al? You said you were going to have a fiddler at the dance and have home . . ."

I beaned Teddy on the head with my tennis racket. Not hard. It's practically brand-new. Just a little tap. The way he hollered and carried on, you'd have thought I killed him. He flopped on the floor, clutching his head and screaming. If he could've figured out a way to create some instant blood, he would've. My mother came into the room and looked at us both.

"Stop that racket," she snapped. "I'm ashamed of you both. Can't you get along for more than ten minutes? Get up off the floor, Teddy."

"She hit me!" Teddy cried. "I wasn't doing anything, and she bopped me on my head."

After my mother had gone, I said through clenched teeth, "How come when you get home trouble starts? How come?"

"Let's see, Ted." Al studied his head as if she were reading a map. "You're fine. Not even a lump. You'll survive."

"I was going to tell you more stuff Mike did," Teddy said, somewhat mollified. "Now I don't think I will."

Al put her arm around him. She's very good with Teddy. He likes Al. She doesn't have to live with him. There are times when I think being an only child is a neat thing. I must remember to tell Al that.

"Don't be a sorehead, Ted," she said, laughing.

"Well." Teddy considered. "We went to Compo Beach on our bikes, and Mike showed us how to find the knotholes in the bathhouses so we could look in at girls undressing."

"Yeah?"

Teddy's crafty little eyes darted from Al's face to mine and back to hers.

"I'd rather put sugar in gas tanks," he said.

"You would?"

"Sure. If you have a sister, seeing a naked girl is no big deal. Mike doesn't have any sisters, so he thinks it is."

I grabbed my tennis racket. "You little weasel!" I shouted, but Teddy was already gone.

CHAPTER 20

"I'll wait outside," I said when we got to the hospital that afternoon. I would've been glad to stand on the street while I waited. I know lots of kids who want to be doctors. Not me. The hospital smell gets to me every time.

"You've got to at least come up with me so my mother can thank you," Al said. "You don't have to hang around if you don't want to." So we each got a card from the admissions office and went up in the elevator.

"I might be in the way," I said, hanging back when we got to Al's mother's room. She pushed me in ahead of her.

"Hello, dear! How nice to see you!" Al's mother said gaily. There was a man sitting in the only chair. He got up as we came in. Oh, oh, I thought. Two's company, three's a crowd, and four's one too many.

"This is Mr. Wright," Al said. We shook hands. He beamed down at me. He wasn't anything like what I expected. He had a jolly round face and his head was freckled and shiny where no hair grew. If he hadn't had on a three-piece suit, he might've passed for a bus driver, I thought.

"I've heard a lot about you and your family," he told me. "And about how kind you've been to Alexandra."

I smiled and tried not to look too wimpy. Sometimes compliments are hard to handle. Mr. Wright wasn't anything like Ole Henry Lynch, Al's mother's former beau.

I went over and kissed Al's mother. Rather, she kissed me. "How are you, dear?" she said. She had dark circles under her eyes and she had lost weight. But otherwise she looked O.K.

"Well, Virginia, I know you want to be alone with these two girls," Mr. Wright said. "So I'll wend my way out. Don't bother seeing me to the door," and he laughed at his own joke. "Doesn't she look first-rate?" he said to Al. "Your mother has weathered the storm. She has come through like a trooper. Get those roses back in her cheeks in jig time. That's the ticket. Get the roses back. Good-bye, Virginia," and Al and I looked on as he gave Al's mother's cheek a little peck. Like a chicken going after grain.

When he'd gone, Al's mother closed her eyes and leaned back against her pillow.

"Are you O.K., Ma?" Al asked anxiously. "Want me to get you a drink of water or anything? Maybe we should go," she said to me.

"No, don't go right this minute." She opened her eyes. "Bill's a dear, really he is. It's just that he wears me out telling me how wonderful I look when I don't feel wonderful. When he's here, I feel as if I had to be cheerful all the time, and it takes something out of me. That's all."

Al went and stood by the bed. "I called Dad and Louise and told them I wouldn't be coming right away," she told her mother. "They said fine, I could come later." Her voice was without expression. No one would've known how much that telephone conversation had cost her.

Tears came to her mother's eyes. I was embarrasssd. I wanted to leave, but my feet stayed where they were.

"I'm proud of you, Alexandra," her mother said. "The way you've stood by me. The way you gave up your trip. I know how much you wanted to go. I know how hard it must've been for you. I remember how important things like that were at your age."

"Hey, Ma!" Al said. "That's what daughters are for. For their poor old mothers to lean on, right?" She tried to make a joke out of it, but both her and her mother's eyes were full of tears. I was on the verge of sneaking out and leaving them alone when Al's mother turned to me and said, "You're a nice child. I'm glad Alexandra has you for a friend."

"Me too," I said.

Al's mother kept smiling at us.

"You are two lovely girls," she said. "Two very nice people. And you've made me very proud." For no reason at all, Mr. Richards popped into my mind. I wondered if he'd popped into Al's.

The nurse bustled in. "Time for our rest," she cried. I wondered if she was going to hop into bed alongside Al's mother and take a rest with her. "Oh, my, haven't we had a lot of visitors this afternoon! And look at all the gorgeous flowers! We certainly did ourselves proud today!"

When we were leaving, Al promised her mother she'd be back tomorrow.

"Tell your mother and father how much I appreciate all they've done," Al's mother said to me. "For Al and me. I'll write to them later. I can never repay them for their kindness."

I said I'd tell them. And we left.

CHAPTER 21

That night Al pushed her dinner around on the plate. Then she asked to be excused from the table. "I don't feel so hot," she said. "My stomach feels peculiar. Maybe if I lie down I'll feel better."

"How about some bicarbonate of soda?" my mother suggested. Al made a face. She hates bicarbonate of soda.

"No, thanks. I'll be fine."

After dessert my father said he was going to play poker with his friends at Mr. Alvord's in 14 F.

"I feel lucky tonight," he said, kissing my mother. "If I win the pot, I might even spring for another night on the town. Keep your fingers crossed, girls."

I asked my mother if she felt like a game of Monopoly. If worse came to worst, we could always let Teddy play. It's better with more people. Except he always breaks down and kicks the chair and snuffles like he's coming down with a cold when he doesn't get Boardwalk. Teddy is a very poor loser.

"Not tonight," she said. "I can't concentrate on all those big real estate deals when it's this hot. Let's talk. We've got a lot of catching up to do."

"Al's mother said she can never repay you and Dad for your kindness," I said. "When we went to see her this afternoon, that's what she said."

"I'm sure she would do the same if I needed her," my mother said. "Bread cast upon the waters. How is she? How did she look?" So I told her about Al's mother getting teary when she told Al she was proud of her for standing by her. I told her about Mr. Wright depressing Al's mother with his cheerfulness. I also told her about the nurse saying, "We certainly did ourselves proud today." My mother likes to hear these little details.

"Poor woman, she's been through a bad time," my mother said. Then I told her about going out to the restaurant with Al and Dad. I told her what we'd had to eat, about the cute waiter, about the kid at the next table with her father and his girl friend. And that the kid wanted to know where my mother was, and I thought she thought my mother was off somewhere getting a divorce and that I was lying when I said my mother was in Connecticut. My mother got a good laugh out of that.

"That was nice of you to share your father with Al," she said. "I can remember, when I was your age, going somewhere alone with my father, which didn't happen very often, was a special thing."

I told her what Al had said, thanking me for making room for her. "I thought that was nice of her to say that," I said. "Dad was terrific. He even told Al it wouldn't have been as nice without her there. That's what he said when she thanked him. I must admit I thought that was going overboard a little," I said. "It would've been perfect with just him and me, but that's what he said. I didn't mind too much. I knew what he meant."

"Your father is a very kind man," my mother said. "I'm sure he had a pretty good idea of what Al was going through, what with her mother in the hospital and her having to postpone her trip. That must've been a tough decision to make."

"I bet she'll never forget that night," I said. "I know I won't."

"Your father told me he'd never enjoyed the company of two young women so much," my mother said.

"He did? He really said that? He called us women?"

She nodded. "He did. And he also said he was proud of you and the way you helped Al over the rough spots.

He said you were made of good stuff and that he was proud you were his daughter."

I was flabbergasted.

"Why didn't he tell me?" I said.

"Because that's not his way. He would tell me but not you. I thought I'd pass it along."

Long after I'd gone to bed I thought about that. Al's mother was proud of her for the way she'd stood by her. Now my father was proud of me for the way I'd acted. Boy. That was pretty nice. I tried to remember if my father had ever been proud of me before. I don't think he ever had. At least if he had been, I didn't know about it.

The next morning Al was already out of bed when I woke up. She was in the kitchen getting breakfast for everybody.

"I'm keeping busy today," she told me grimly. "So I won't think what day it is."

It was the day she was supposed to go to the farm. Right this minute she should be taxiing down the runway on her way to the farm, the barn dance, the homemade ice cream, never mind Louise, the boys, her father. And Brian. That was a lot of stuff to give up.

Then Al's mother called. She was thrilled. A man she knew in Small Appliances had heard she was sick, and he had called her to offer her the use of his beach cottage on the Jersey Shore. He and his wife were going to Toledo to see their grandson. So she and Al could go there after she got out of the hospital. Wasn't that great?

"Yeah, that's great," Al muttered. "But I know her. Give her a shot of sea air and she'll start making noises about going back to work. I'm going to have to crack the whip, tell her what she can and can't do for a while. You've got to watch her."

"That's neat," I said. "You'll have a real vacation." I tried not to sound wistful. She gave me a piercer.

"Maybe you could come along with us," Al said. "I'll ask." I thought about that. I would love to go to the Jersey Shore. But not this time. This was Al's time for her to get to know her mother better, to take care of her and for them to relax, just the two of them. I knew I'd be in the way. People have to have time to themselves. Last week I wouldn't have known that. It seemed to me I'd matured a lot in a few days. I have to live up to my father's pride in me.

"Don't ask her," I said to Al. "Don't put her on the spot. It wouldn't be fair."

"What wouldn't be fair?" Teddy hung around, watching us.

"Why don't you go play with your friend Hubie?" I said. I hate it when he hangs around with his mouth hanging open like that.

"Hubie's away." Teddy picked at a scab on his knee until part of it came off. He ate the part he'd pulled off.

"Stop that!" I shouted. "That's disgusting!"

"You ever eat a scab?" he said nonchalantly. "It doesn't taste bad. Sort of like fried chicken. Not the kind your mother makes. The kind you eat at home. I mean the kind you buy at a fried chicken restaurant."

"Nice, Ted," Al said. "Very nice."

"All it is is your own dried skin," Teddy said, chewing. "Hubie asked me to visit him."

I turned. "When?"

"Next week. His mother said he could have a friend and he picked me. I just got home and now I'm off again." Teddy lifted both hands, palms up, and smiled complacently at us.

"Close your mouth," I ordered. "You'll catch a lot of flies that way. They might get stuck in your throat and you'd strangle to death."

"Hubie's house is right on the ocean," Teddy said in a sugary voice. "All we do is fall out of bed and onto the beach and into the ocean."

I bugged my eyes out as far as they'd go and still stay in their sockets.

"You mean where they have those enormous waves? And those man-eating sharks? *That* ocean?"

Teddy ducked his head and sucked nervously on what was left of his scab.

"And that undertow!" I cried. "I've heard tales of that undertow, how it can pull an experienced swimmer miles down the beach. How it takes people out to the middle of the ocean, practically to Portugal. I wonder if Mom knows about that undertow. If she knew, she probably wouldn't let you go. I better go tell her," and I started toward the door.

"Quit it!" Teddy howled. "You're just jealous! If someone asked you to go to the ocean, boy, I bet you'd break a leg getting there. That's all you are is jealous." He left in a huff.

He hadn't been gone more than a couple of seconds when I said in a loud voice, "You never did tell me what an all-in-one is, Al. Or a C-H-A-S-T-I-T-Y belt either."

There are two things you can be sure of when it comes to Teddy. One is that he's out there eavesdropping. Two is that when you spell a word out, he's absolutely sure it's something he's not supposed to know. That gives him fits. I figured it was time for him to have a few fits. Going away twice in one month while I sat home twiddling my thumbs.

"Well," Al said slowly, tugging at her skirt, "an all-in-one is . . ." and she let her voice dangle in midair.

"I know!" Teddy came screeching around the corner. "Let me tell! Let me tell!" he hollered.

Al and I rolled our eyes at each other.

"O.K., Ted," she said, "tell us."

Teddy planted his feet wide apart and locked his hands behind his back as if he were about to recite a long poem.

"This oughta be good," Al murmured.

"An all-in-one," Teddy explained, "is when a guy hits the golf ball and it goes VROOM!" Teddy is big on sound effects. "It goes flying through the air with the speed of light and it lands smack in the hole. Smack into this tiny little hole with the flag sticking out of it that he's aiming for. That's what they call an all-in-one," Teddy said. He stood back, studying our faces, waiting and watching our reaction to his story.

A stunned silence fell.

"So that's what an all-in-one is," I said at last.

Teddy's eyes darted from Al's face to mine, then back to Al's. "How about it, Al?" he asked her. "Isn't that right?"

She went over to him and put her hand on his head. "Ted," she said, her voice filled with emotion, "when they made you, they threw away the mold."

Teddy's lips curved in a tentative smile.

"That's right," he finally said, deciding Al wasn't pulling his leg. "They made me and they threw away the mold. You said it." He gave Al a huge thump on the back that made her eyes water.

"You said a mouthful, baby!" he shouted. "Don't give me no flak, either, baby!" and he sailed out of the room on his way to conquer the ocean and the undertow and the sharks.

"All-in-one, hole-in-one, *quelle différence*?" Al said philosophically.

When I was absolutely sure he was gone, I said to Al, "Just exactly what is an all-in-one?"

"A foundation garment," she told me, "worn by

ladies with full figures. To keep them in shape."

"Who wears them?"

"Some of my mother's customers," Al said. "Ladies who buy Better Dresses. Who else?"

Next morning the doorbell rang. "Who could that be?" my mother said. Teddy beat her to the door.

We heard a man's voice say, "Air Mail, Special Delivery. Sign here please."

"It's for you, Al!" Teddy hollered. "It's a big envelope for you."

"Well, bring it here, wimp," I called.

Al is one of those maddening people who studies a package before she opens it. She turned this big thick envelope one way, then another. She shook it and put it to her ear. The only thing she *didn't* do was smell it.

"Who's it from?" my mother said.

Teddy was breathing down Al's neck. "Open it, open it," he said, clutching himself as if he had to go to the bathroom. He probably did.

"The postmark's Chillicothe, Ohio," Al said in a tone of wonder. "That's where the farm is. Chillicothe, Ohio."

"For Pete's sake," I shouted, "it's from your father. Open it before I kill you."

She did, but slowly, so slowly I couldn't stand it. "You must be a real winner on Christmas morning," I told her.

She took out something dark blue. "What is it?" she said a few times. She held up something that looked like a huge T-shirt.

"Cool," she said in a puzzled way.

"It has writing on it," I said. "Shake it out and see what it says."

Al stood up so she could get a better look. It was a very large T-shirt. On the front was spelled out AL(ex-andra) THE GREAT.

"Not to be confused with Alexander the Great," my mother said. "That's terrific. Here's a note, Al. It fell out when you pulled out your present." She handed Al a slip of paper. Al read aloud:

> *"To Al. This says it in a nutshell. You are great. We love you and will see you soon. Dad and Louise and Nick, Chris, and Sam."*

"What a nice present," my mother said. "And they're right, Al."

"Put it on," I told her. "See how it fits."

"It's gigantic," she said, giggling. Al almost never giggles, so I knew this was a big moment. She put on the T-shirt over what she already had on. She looked really fat.

My mother went out of the room. "Who in heck was Alexander the Great?" Al whispered. "I know I should know, but I don't, and I didn't want to let on when your mother said that."

"Here you are." My mother plunked down the encyclopedia on the dining room table. "Look him up. This will tell you everything you want to know about Alexander the Great."

"Wow," I said after we'd read Alexander the Great's credentials. "Talk about being a real winner."

It seemed that Alexander the Great, a.k.a. Alexander the Third, born 356 B.C., died 323 B.C. (I always like the way those B.C. dates go backwards), was one of the greatest leaders, not to mention generals and warriors, of all time. He was king of Macedonia and conquered almost all of Asia. When he wasn't routing Persian forces, he was defeating anything and anyone that got in his way. Old Alexander the Great was a star. From start to finish. A real achiever. And he died when he was only thirty-three.

"Boy," Al mused, "if that guy were alive today, he'd be the president of about ten corporations already. Do you think they're trying to tell me something? Dad and Louise, I mean? Do you think they're trying to tell me to get off my duff and conquer something?"

"No," I said. "I think they're trying to tell you they think you're great. That you did something heroic when you said you couldn't make the barn dance. That's what I think."

Al looked at me in a dazed way. Her eyes glittered as if they were made of bits of glass.

"You are young but very wise, my friend," she said. "You are wise beyond your years." And she hugged the T-shirt to her chest, smiling.

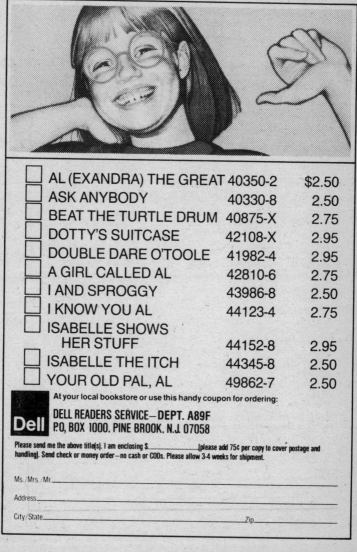